HAUNTS
of
CRUELTY

R.S. CROW

To those who cry in the dark, and no one hears.

"The dark places of the earth
are full of the haunts of cruelty."
—Psalm 74:20, NKJV

HAUNTS
of
CRUELTY

Book Two in *The Brothers Series*

Part One

1

Jeremiah and Bri rest body to body in their wicker love seat, watching the morning. To them, the early peace of a quiet dawn is worth a little less sleep, and provides time together as husband and wife before daily roles demand their attention. They barely say a word. They sit quietly. Elbows on her thighs, Bri grips her steaming coffee mug, while Jeremiah brushes his fingertips across her back.

Across the way, Caroline steps out from her home, dressed in her blue nurses' uniform and white sneakers so clean they appear bright. Along the front path, Caroline bends at her gardenia bush to enjoy the fragrance from a single white bud. Her eyes close. She shakes her head in subtlety, as if falling back into a memory she forgot about far too long. She stands again. Bri and Jeremiah watch with absent attention as Caroline rolls her trashcan to the curb at the end of her driveway.

Jeremiah calls out with a wave, "Good morning."

The greeting goes unreturned.

Jeremiah's hand wilts, returning to the other side of his coffee mug, heat on his palm and fingers.

With a tender grin, Bri offers in consolation, "She probably couldn't hear you over the sound of the trashcan." Rubbing her slippered feet together, Bri then draws them beneath her body for warmth against the cool breeze.

Jeremiah says, "No, she was ignoring me. She's probably thinking in her head, 'Wow, that guy really sucks.'"

Bri laughs, glancing at her husband's dark eyes and offers, "She doesn't think you suck, hon'."

"She does."

Bri reconsiders. "Yeah, you're probably right."

Caroline notices the couple across her way, then calls out with a smile as bright as her shoes, "Good morning, you two."

"Good morning," Bri returns. Jeremiah offers a wave only shoulder high, mouth at his mug as his narrow eyes peek through the dark strands of hair dangling over his brow. He can't help but feel pouty.

Caroline asks, "How're those beautiful babies?"

"Getting bigger every day," Bri responds.

"I know that's right, Sugar! Keep feeding them like you do! You two go on and have a great day now. I'm going to get on to work."

A moment later, Caroline drives past with one last wave.

Jeremiah shakes his head. "Yep, she did that on purpose."

"Did what?"

"Pretended not to hear me, and then just talked to you."

"Yeah, you're probably right." Bri smiles. Resting beside him, Bri touches her husband's hand and interlaces her fingers with his.

Another breeze brushes the porch, bringing goose bumps to the exposed skin of Bri's arms. She shivers, pressing herself further into her husband's side. The way she's positioned, along with the chill of the morning, reminds Jeremiah of camping – as though Bri might be in the woods sitting before the smoldering ashes of a previous night's fire as mountain air resides in coldness between the trees. Jeremiah hopes more than anything that Bri doesn't read his mind in her wifely way and ask about camping sometime soon. He hates camping, and would prefer to avoid it for as long as possible. He tries to think about something else.

They continue to watch the cul-de-sac awaken for the day as it's hoisted up by the grips of morning. They've enjoyed this place – this little corner of the world – where their home and neighborhood have been as good and right as Baby Bear's porridge and chair. It is a home that has heard the infant cries of each of their three children and has witnessed the evidence of age starting to show on the young parent's faces.

Bri yawns out in exclamation, "Oh, my goodness."

2

Jeremiah asks, "Cole up again last night?"

Finishing the yawn, Bri says, "Actually, it was Gavin."

Jeremiah states with concern, "He's having nightmares lately."

"I know."

Jeremiah thinks about the nightmares his son is having. He's unsure of how to console his eldest son because he can't remember when the Boogieman became less threatening to himself when he was a child. There was never a word that helped, and any assurance from his own parents that it was just his imagination only emboldened such fears, made them more alive. He refuses to impart such lies to Gavin. He admits, "I'm not sure how to help him."

"Gavin has an imagination like yours. He dreams like you."

"I know." Jeremiah is sorry for the truth of it.

Another neighbor, Stan, exits his front door, wearing a tattered shirt meant for lawn work and car repairs, stained with evidence of such things. With a huff of irritation, Stan snatches up a shredded trash bag that has been ripped apart by local raccoons – a group of them have been causing mischief recently like a band of teenage delinquents. Stan shakes his head, then gathers up the scattered trash one piece at a time. He kicks macaroni into the grass, which a couple of crows turn their heads to from the light post nearby. Finished, Stan then rumbles his trashcan down the driveway, bending back to counter the weight.

Jeremiah waits until the rumbling stops before offering a morning greeting, this time using the name to ensure a catching of Stan's ears. "Good morning, Stan!"

Again, the greeting falls flat. Bri laughs at the sour expression of her husband. She then laughs harder while teasing, "It's okay, hon'."

"I am a really terrible greeter," Jeremiah concludes with a grin.

"You're not a terrible greeter. Our neighbors just hate you."

He laughs. "Yeah, you're probably right." His tone hints that he knew it the whole time, and he smiles even bigger at the continued amusement of his wife.

Stan is at his mailbox, touching the flowerbed with a boot. Noticing the couple sitting on the front porch, he calls out with a southern twang, "Good morning, y'all!"

"Good morning!" Jeremiah bursts out joyously, as though he's never been greeted before in his entire life and is excited by the newness of such a thing, sitting up and stretching over the railing as if he's about to burst over the edge.

"Good morning!" Bri only partially gets out as she stifles another laugh.

Before Stan can inquire about what's so funny, Jeremiah asks, "Raccoons get into your trash again last night?"

"Nope."

Jeremiah pauses, still against the railing, too baffled to respond before Stan returns into his own home.

"What was that all about?" Jeremiah asks as he sits again.

"What do you mean?"

"It's pretty obvious raccoons got into his trash."

"I don't know. Maybe he thinks you're teasing him."

Jeremiah says, "Maybe he thinks I did it."

Bri agrees, "Probably."

"I just can't get enough of other people's trash."

"That's true. It's one of the things I love about you."

Jeremiah laughs. "Well, at least someone does."

The screen door opens to their right. Gavin stumbles out, holding his faded blue blanket to his face, the tip of it dragging behind him as he steps out onto the porch.

Placing her coffee cup atop the railing, Bri greets, "Good morning, sleepyhead." She pulls Gavin into her arms.

Gavin peeks at his father from over Bri's shoulder as he rests against her. The boy offers a muffled greeting through his blanket and into his mother's shirt, "Good morning, Papa."

Jeremiah touches his son's hair. "Good morning."

Gavin's eyes reveal the hidden smile.

Jeremiah asks, "Where's your brother?"

"Still sleeping."

Bri cautions, "Okay, good. Let's not wake him up."

Gavin says, "Abigail's awake though. She was talking in her crib."

"Okay, good." Bri passes Gavin over to Jeremiah as she stands. She grabs up the two empty coffee mugs and says, "That girl has been sleeping really good lately. I'm going to get her and feed her something."

"Okay."

The screen door shuts. Jeremiah and Gavin sit together.

The air steadily warms as the morning spreads around them. Gavin asks his father questions of the world, pointing to trees and bushes and birds and flying bugs that fill their little piece of the neighborhood. Jeremiah answers his son as best he can. After a short while, Jeremiah says, "I have to get ready for work."

"Okay."

"Do you want me to make you a bagel or oatmeal for breakfast?"

Gavin answers, "A bagel."

4

"Okay." Jeremiah stands with his son wrapped in his arms and declares, "Some day, you'll carry me around and make me bagels."

Gavin smiles. "Okay, Papa."

At the door, Jeremiah's hand stops at the bronzed handle as Gavin calls out, "Uncle Langdon is here." The boy straightens with excitement as he points towards the street. Langdon zips into the cul-de-sac. His car clinks and clanks to a halt in front of the mailbox with a squeal of the brakes. Langdon steps out and turns his broad back to them as he reaches across to the passenger seat. He then presents a wide box of donuts and kicks the door shut behind him with a smile of greeting.

"Donuts!" Gavin calls, putting a bigger smile on Langdon's face. The boy squirms and Jeremiah places him down. Gavin runs and hugs Langdon's thigh as Langdon raises the boxes to allow Gavin to fit beneath.

"Hey," Langdon greets with Gavin still at his side.

"Hey." Jeremiah smiles.

Gavin declares, "Uncle Langdon brought donuts."

"I can see that."

The front door of the home is pushed open, bouncing at the end of its chain as Cole shoves out onto the porch. The young boy's body stands sure and solid as he yells, "Donuts! Uncle Langdon brought donuts!"

Langdon smiles. "I feel like the Queen of England."

"At my house, you are the Queen of England," Jeremiah assures.

"Sweet."

"What?" Cole asks loudly as he nears.

"Nothing," Jeremiah says.

Langdon asks, "You headed to work soon?"

"Yeah. Have to be there by 9."

"Okay. I wasn't planning on staying long, but I've been doing terrible on my diet, so I figured I could at least try and make you fat."

Jeremiah smirks, tall and lean beside his friend. "Good thinking."

"It's a pretty solid plan."

Cole declares again, "Uncle Langdon, you brought donuts."

"Yes, I did." Langdon drops to scoop Cole up. The boy wraps his arms around Langdon's muscular neck as Langdon lifts him. The four of them go inside.

In the kitchen, Bri turns at the sink with the water running from the faucet as she rinses a bowl and scolds, "No donuts until after breakfast, Uncle Langdon."

Jeremiah pauses, caught with a donut in his mouth. The two boys offer their mother looks of pleading and Cole declares, "But Papa said we could."

5

Langdon grabs a donut and assures with a wink, "Yeah, Papa said we could."

Jeremiah apologizes to his wife with a grin, and she shakes her head in defeat at the simple way her husband's charm can disarm her. "Fine," she says.

Heads at the counter, the two boys reach inside the box. Donuts in hand, their eyes are big with expectation as they walk into the dining room. The adults stay in the kitchen, talking about grown up things.

The brothers climb onto their chairs, sitting beside each other at the table. Icing colors expand around their mouths in pink and blue as Abigail smiles in her highchair, swatting her spoon around as she sends oatmeal flying. Jeremiah comes in not too long after. He kisses each of them before saying goodbye. Standing at the window, Gavin waves as Jeremiah drives away, and Cole mimics his older brother as he stands beside him.

2

The window ceiling of the car dealership reveals the blue sky pierced by the singleness of the shimmering sun. Jeremiah watches the clouds pass over with the busyness of the dealership humming around about him. The printer slides back and forth methodically, pushing pages out and providing Jeremiah with the list of vehicles he is to photograph. Taking his eyes from the daydream above, Jeremiah turns his attention to the sales lot outside, preparing himself for what the new shipment looks like, hoping there aren't too many vans with their countless features and options, the newest of them easily needing twice the amount of pictures of any other car. The printer spits out another sheet. The stack growing. It's going to be a long day.

The April air sneaks inside the building with the brief and repeated openings of the double door entrance, bringing in hints of warmth and new flowers, bumblebees and bird songs. It's a day for family walks and strollers. A day for easy conversations and smiles. For resolutions to be a better person. Jeremiah watches as a family of four comes in. The faces of the two children hold wide eyes of wonder at how big the building is, how shiny and new. The parents glance around in expectation as well, eyeing the cars parked inside for display. Jeremiah studies the father as though the man were in a catalogue. The father appears mild-natured and pleasant, with a caring smile that remains there for his children as they ask questions with fingers pointing. The man answers them with patience. His smile doesn't waver. Jeremiah wishes he were more like that. More kind in nature. But his sharp features alone make him feel as though he could never pretend to be such a way. So easily gentle.

Jeremiah has been trying though. To be what he ought to be. He's been more focused on being positive, making an effort to control and improve upon his dark and shaky temperament. He wants to provide himself to his children as someone who is always there for them, and not just on the good days. The effort has felt much like walking a tightrope, arms out to stay balanced. Some days are better. Some are not. He fails more than he succeeds.

A few weeks ago, Bri begged him out of desperation, "Jeremiah, please. You need to control your moods." She was right. He was wearing on her, and he knew it. And if on her, then surely on his children. It has caused him to look in the mirror each morning to remind himself of how he must be. In control. Not slipping off to that dark place. An appeal. A shaking of the shoulders to always remember.

"Have all you need?" Emad, the owner, asks as he approaches.

Jeremiah turns with a smile as he straightens up and answers, "Yes, I do. I'm just waiting for the printer to finish and I'll get right to it."

"This printer is far too slow. I will buy a new one." Emad pulls the sheets out as they finish up, his part in being helpful to his employees. He places the stack into Jeremiah's waiting hand and makes request with his Persian accent, "Try and have these done by lunch. We have another shipment coming, and I want to have them all photographed before the end of the work day. You can do this?"

Jeremiah assures, "I'll get them done as soon as possible."

While scanning over the room for anything out of place or order, Emad replies, "Perfect," his common answer to anything that meets his approval. With a strong grip on Jeremiah's shoulder, Emad asks, "How's your beautiful family?" as if he had not just been speaking of time and duty.

"They're great." Jeremiah scoops up the camera from the desk.

"Perfect." Emad turns his attention over to Komyar who scans his computer for auction deals. Interrupting him, Emad speaks to Komyar about a problem he's upset with. The two of them argue heatedly in Farsi. Komyar defends himself and his ability to do his job. Emad says it's not good enough. Cutting off the debate, Emad walks away, leaving Komyar stumbling in mid-sentence.

Komyar sighs heavily. He says to Jeremiah, "Sheesh, you'd think that guy just hired me. He acts as if I don't know what I'm doing."

"He loves you," Jeremiah offers with a grin.

Komyar laughs in good cheer. "You're right, buddy. You'd just think after a vacation he'd come back more at ease or something."

Jeremiah considers this for a moment. "That's not how Emad is. He's a great boss though."

"He is." Komyar dips his face back to the computer. He nods in approval of something, then lifts his attention back to Jeremiah while brushing a hand over his sleek hair. "Why do you do that?"

"Do what?"

"You always say Emad is a great boss."

"I just think he's a good man. Besides, people are always complaining about things. And I don't want to be like them."

Komyar brightens. "That's good, buddy," he says, as if making a mental note to be more like that himself, despite his cheerful disposition.

"See you soon," Jeremiah says with a smile.

"Get it done, buddy."

Jeremiah walks towards the entrance with the camera. He props open the door for a customer who scuttles forward with a thank you left in the entryway. Outside, Jeremiah pulls in a deep breath. His lungs fill with the air, eyes closed as the sun warms him. He decides immediately that he'll start with the BMW 5 series – a perfect fit for a perfect morning. "This will help me be a more positive person," he states with a smile to himself, shuffling between a pair of parked cars.

Jeremiah finishes the photographs just before noon. His footfalls echo over the marbled tile of the dealership as he walks out of the sales office where he uploaded pictures to the dealership website.

"Hey there, buddy," Komyar greets. "Get those pictures done? Emad was asking."

"Done." Jeremiah places the camera atop the counter.

"Perfect," Komyar says.

"Perfect."

Komyar asks, "So, you liked that new BMW I brought in? You were gone for a while." He winks.

Jeremiah hopes no one else noticed, and he sneaks his head left and right as though knowing faces may be looking at him from behind corners. He whispers, "It was fantastic."

"Perfect."

"Perfect."

Emad's direct assistant, Hannah, walks towards them. Her heels click out a brisk pace in demonstration of her ongoing impatience with those around her. She looks annoyed as always. Despite her youth and attractiveness, it causes her to lose much of her beauty. Komyar's eyes brighten as she joins them – as his eyes brighten for everyone – and he greets, "Well, hello, Ms. Hannah. For what do we owe the pleasure?"

Ignoring the pleasantry, Hannah explains, "Terrell's birthday is coming up. Emad wants me to get him a card and a small gift to make him feel welcome as a new team member. I don't know what to get him. Do either of you know what he likes? Maybe one of you can finally be useful."

"Tennis," Jeremiah answers immediately, as though Terrell and Tennis were meant to be together. Terrell with sweat bands and high socks skidding back and forth over the tennis court of victory.

"Tennis?" Hannah asks in skepticism.

Jeremiah assures, "He loves tennis."

"*He loves tennis?*"

Jeremiah accuses, "You think he doesn't like tennis because he's black. That's racist, Hannah."

Hannah takes a half-step back from the accusation as she scrambles with her words. "No. No. He likes tennis. That's great. I'll get him something that has to do with tennis."

Jeremiah offers, "That's a good idea."

Komyar says, "I used to play tennis. Great sport. It was the first thing I enjoyed recreationally after coming here from Iran."

Jeremiah nods, always enjoying Komyar's stories of new life in America, as though it were a reincarnation – a reincarnation that permitted him to play tennis.

Hannah states, "No one cares, Komyar."

Jeremiah corrects, "I care, Komyar."

Komyar's smile beams. "Thanks, buddy."

"Like I said, 'no one cares,'" Hannah repeats.

Terrell approaches, looking nervous. He asks Jeremiah, "Emad wants to know if the pictures are done. Please tell me you did them."

"They're done. I uploaded them about fifteen minutes ago."

"Great!" Terrell shakes his head as if just narrowly avoiding some grave misfortune. "Emad said he was going to have me do it if you hadn't. He said they had to get done by 1:00 o'clock. Last thing I want is to start off on the wrong foot with Emad. I need this job and I have no idea how to do the pictures. I don't want him to think he can't depend on me, you know."

Jeremiah assures, "You're fine. It's good actually. It means Emad trusts you to follow up on things."

Komyar nods. "Yep, that's true."

Jeremiah then says, "Terrell, did you know that Hannah thought you would never play tennis because you're black?"

"What?! No! That is *not* what I said!" Hannah asserts.

Terrell looks at them all with confusion. "I don't play tennis."

Jeremiah states, "That's not the point. Hannah didn't think you would ever play tennis. She guessed you played basketball or football."

Terrell nods. "I used to play both in high school. Now I just play pickup basketball games with my boys."

Hannah glares at Jeremiah, prepared to depart with a fist full of vindication, but Jeremiah restrains her steps as he says, "Hannah also said you played, *Prison Ball*."

Komyar bursts out laughing. Jeremiah chuckles, unable to resist.

Finally seeing that this has nothing to do with tennis, but is all about teasing Hannah, Terrell laughs, then repeats, "*Prison Ball*," like it's the funniest thing he's heard in a while. Like he can finally smile naturally here at work because these people aren't so bad. Terrell walks away, announcing that he has to detail a few more cars and repeating again, "Prison ball," with a laugh.

Komyar scolds, "Hannah! Prison Ball! You should be ashamed!"

"Shut-up, Komyar, and get back to work!" It's all Hannah can seem to say before clicking away.

Unthreatened by the young lovely lady and her threats and attempts at intimidation, Komyar smiles with a sip of coffee, shaking his head with the enjoyment of the moment as it has provided them all a break from serious matters. Komyar watches as Jeremiah walks out through the front doors to help customers for the afternoon. He hopes Jeremiah finds the Jeep SRT-8 he ordered, almost more for Jeremiah's enjoyment than for any customer who might purchase it. Chuckling again, Komyar repeats, "'Prison ball,'" as he views another auction.

3

"You're home early," Bri says as she peeks up from the kitchen counter, her face bright with a smile of surprise as her husband enters through the garage door entryway an hour before expected. Bri's apron is dusted and spotted. Cooking utensils in both hands. The kitchen is alive with the smells of garlic and spices. Aromas of a homemade dinner.

"Yep," Jeremiah responds with a smile of his own. He tosses his keys atop the table to his left – a wedding gift from years ago. Pictures of family greet Jeremiah on the wall as he walks to the counter that divides the kitchen. "What are you making? It smells delicious." He then says, "You look pretty hot like that."

"I look hot like this?" Bri's cheeks redden with a dash of embarrassment as she stands in flour dustings, her body tired after a draining day of chasing children.

Bri runs a cherry tomato through a bowl of homemade pesto and offers it to Jeremiah as he comes around the counter, "Here." She drops it into his open mouth. Jeremiah nods with approval as he chews with a garbled proclamation of, "delicious." Grabbing another tomato, he plasters it in pesto, gobbling it down as well. "What's pesto made of anyway?" Jeremiah asks, a third cherry tomato being coated.

"Leave some for later," Bri scolds as she seals the Tupperware container before sliding it into the refrigerator. Bri counts out the ingredients on her fingers as she lists them. "Walnuts, basil, olive oil, Parmesan cheese, salt and pepper, and lemon juice."

Jeremiah adds, "Garlic," his mouth full of the unmistakable potency.

"Garlic. Lots of garlic."

Jeremiah says, "I should probably be on Hell's Kitchen. Chef Ramsey would be super impressed with my palate. He'd probably say, *'Jeremiah! You have an amazing palate! You Muppet! Donkey!'*"

"Yes, he would dear. He would be sooooo impressed. As long as it was garlic he was testing you on."

"Yep. Actually, I dreamt about him last night."

She laughs. "Chef Ramsey?"

"Yep."

"You would."

"Yep." He says, "I was driving on a bridge and he was guiding traffic like a policeman. When he saw me, he got into my car and we drove off to a baseball game."

Bri says, "You hate baseball."

Jeremiah assures, "I'd go to a baseball game with Chef Ramsey though."

"But not with me."

"Nope. Just Chef Ramsey."

Jeremiah pulls his wife into a hug and holds her close. He then lifts her, squeezing her tight. She wraps her legs around his waist. They kiss, garlic on their faces. Jeremiah then kisses her more passionately, hands low on her back, but she cautions, "The boys are in the living room."

"So?"

"So –" but Bri has no answer. Her feet touch the floor. "Save the fun for later."

Jeremiah turns to find his children, but before he can leave, Bri places a jar in his path. "Can you open this?"

"Sure."

Bri explains, "I asked Stan to open it, but he couldn't."

A disgruntled expression peels out over Jeremiah's face as territorial disdain crinkles his forehead and tightens his eyes. He asks, "You asked Stan?"

"Yeah, I needed it open and he was home." She teases, "Why? Are you jealous?"

"Nope. I know you love me."

"I do." She goes to kiss him, but stops, leaving Jeremiah leaning forward with expectant lips as she explains, "You have to open it first."

Jeremiah grips the bottom firmly, then the top, but before he can begin, Bri asks, "Do you want a towel for a better grip?"

He sighs out gruffly. "Jeez. Stop interrupting me. No. I don't need a towel." And he twists, his strong slender forearms rippling as he does. A loud "pop!" smacks out from the jar. Jeremiah presents the open container.

"You've got to be kidding me!"

"I can understand you not opening it, with your frail woman wrists and all, but Stan?"

"Hey, he tried. And my wrists aren't frail."

Jeremiah offers, "Maybe Stan is actually a woman."

"Maybe," Bri agrees with a roll of her eyes as she turns and pours the contents into the crockpot of chicken and broth and spices.

A triumphant smile arises on Jeremiah's face. He feels like Gaston, standing tall and proud, swinging from chandeliers with biceps and arm hair. He sings out while twirling through the kitchen, "No one opens jars like Gaston, opens jars like Gaston, opens jars like Gaston, in a jar opening match no one opens jars like Gaston!" He takes Bri up by the hips, attempting to swing her around with him, but she brushes him off while commenting, "Your song is a little redundant there, hon'."

"Hey, Papa! What are you doing here?" Gavin comes into the kitchen, his dirty blond hair tossed in front of his eyes and a smile on his face.

"I live here!" Jeremiah answers in a melody as he pulls Gavin up to swing him in continued dancing circles. He calls out over Gavin's shoulder, "Come here, Cole!"

"Okay!" Cole yells from the other room. The clattering sound of dropped plastic toys is heard, followed by Cole's pattering feet as his bowed legs sprint him into the kitchen.

Scooping him up, Jeremiah kisses Cole, but Cole shies away. "Papa! Don't kiss me!" he commands.

"Oh, and why not?"

"I'm not a girl!" Cole declares in answer.

"That's true. But you're my son, and I'll always give you kisses. Even when you're bigger than me, I'll still give you kisses."

"Ugh, okay, Papa." The boy turns, his lips puckered as he braces for a kiss.

With Gavin scooped up in his left arm and Cole in his right, Jeremiah stands with both sons and places one more kiss on each of them.

Gavin says, "You kiss Mommy too."

Jeremiah nods. "Yep," with a sly grin as he lays eyes on his wife who smiles back at her sassy husband.

Gavin states, "And sometimes you kiss mommy with tongue."

Jeremiah laughs.

"Hey! How'd you know that?" Bri's cheeks blush.

"I saw you," he says.

"When?"

"I don't know."

"When?" Bri asks again.

Gavin answers, "When Papa was leaving this morning."

Jeremiah promises, "I thought no one was looking. I guess I need to clean up my kissing tactics."

"I guess so." Bri points a spatula at him.

"Papa, I want to get down, I want to go play Angry Birds," Cole announces as he wriggles in Jeremiah's arm.

Placing both sons back to the kitchen floor, Jeremiah announces, "No Angry Birds. You two, go outside. It's beautiful," and before they can protest, he says, "and no crying about it."

"But we were outside a lot already today," Gavin says.

"Good. Then you can spend more time outside with me. I'm going to talk with Momma a little bit more, and then we'll walk up to the lake to throw rocks."

"The lake?" Gavin asks with excitement.

"Yep."

"Okay," Gavin says in agreement.

Cole says, "I'm not going, Papa."

"Yeah, you are." Jeremiah grins, already prepared for Cole's opposition.

"I don't want to. I want to play Angry Birds."

"Too bad. I'm bigger than you."

Cole stomps angrily on his way out, thumping in loud rebellion.

Jeremiah shakes his head with a smile. He asks his wife, "Where's Abigail?"

"She's still napping."

"Should I go get her?"

"Almost. You can take her to the lake with you."

"That's what I was thinking. She loves it."

"Give her ten more minutes for her nap."

"Perfect." Jeremiah asks, "How was she today?"

"Abigail?"

"Of course."

"She was good."

"Did she start doing any new baby tricks?"

Bri crosses her arms as the crockpot bubbles behind her. She recounts, "Well, earlier in the morning Gavin was killing flies at the window. I later found Abigail with a fly on her lip and two other flies in her fist. She had been eating the flies Gavin had killed!"

Jeremiah pictures his baby daughter sitting on the floor with her big blue eyes, a dead fly dangling from her lip. He's almost proud. "That's awesome."

Bri pours some wine. "It's disgusting."

"It's kind of cool."

"No, it's really not."

"Just a little bit."

"No. It's not."

Jeremiah offers, "I'll have a talk with her later about it."

"She's only eight months old," Bri corrects, wine glass resting against her chest.

Jeremiah acts out: "'Abigail, you can't eat flies because Mommy thinks it's super-duper gross. I think it's cool, but your mother doesn't.' Abigail will be all like, '*hehmeeh*.'" Jeremiah mimics out Abigail's simple new phrase with a surprised expression on his face, looking ridiculous on a man with beginning creases along his eyes as he impersonates his baby girl. Bri laughs comically, feigning amusement, then punches Jeremiah in the stomach. Jeremiah coughs out a laugh. "Good thing you punch like a girl."

She slugs him again, this time harder. "I am a girl!"

He chortles, "That one hurt."

"Good." The stress of the day has melted away with the comforting presence of her husband, the wine also doing its fair part. Bri relaxes further as she says, "I'm glad you're home."

Jeremiah enjoys her words, like a small burden released. "It's good to be home." He then assures, "I've been trying to control my moods more. I have."

"I know. I've noticed."

"After what happened with the scissors, I promise, nothing like that will ever happen again."

"I know." Bri takes him in her arms, assuring Jeremiah all is forgiven. "I love you. Even with your moods."

Jeremiah tilts an ear to the ceiling. "I hear Abigail."

"Okay, good."

"I'll go get her."

"Make sure you change her diaper."

"Of course." Jeremiah says, "Then I'll take them all up to the lake to skip rocks."

"Sounds good. Dinner will be ready in about an hour."

Jeremiah kisses Bri again. He walks up the stairs towards his daughter's room. The young girl is yelling, not crying, for someone to acknowledge that she's awake, and Jeremiah smiles at that. Opening the door to his daughter's bedroom, she shakes the wooden guard of the crib at the sight of him, smiling a toothless smile as he comes closer. Holding her, carrying her, Jeremiah finds himself filled with thankfulness for his wife and his children as they pull his pieces together, forming him into something he never was. He kisses his girl. "Let's go to the lake."

"Hehmeeh," she says to him.

"Hehmeeh." He kisses her again.

4

A crack of thunder shakes the windows and sends a shudder through Gavin's shoulders as he sits on the living room floor. He shivers, staring at the ceiling and the walls as though they've betrayed him. Abigail cries out in a burst of fear, lifting her arms into the air to show her want of being lifted into stronger arms. Jeremiah reaches down as her tiny fingers stretch for him, her round blue eyes filled with tiny tears. Jeremiah embraces her with whispers of comfort. She softens against him.

Cole doesn't seem to notice the ongoing acts of angry thunder, even as the lights shake and the windows thrum again in vibration. The boy continues to play atop the carpeted floor with Iron-Man in one hand and Woody in another, much to Woody's dismay as Iron Man slams the lanky and floppy cowboy against the coffee table. "Ooooooph! Aaaaah! Ouch!" Cole mixes the battle cries and grunts of the two toys, finishing with Iron-Man declaring, "Give up, Woody! You are a bad bad guy!"

Jeremiah explains, "Cole, they're both good guys."

"Ooooph, ouch!" Cole keeps his attention fixed on the action as he contradicts his father, "No, Papa! Woody is a bad Woody!"

"Well then, I guess he's just getting what he deserves."

Iron Man is further emboldened by the declaration of Jeremiah, and he flings bad Woody across the room where he hits the wall, slumping down with his arms sprawled out and legs over his head.

Jeremiah asks Gavin, "Want to go outside and watch the storm?"

Gavin nods with his blanket to his mouth.

"Good." Jeremiah smiles. He then asks, "Cole, want to go sit on the porch and watch the storm with us?"

Cole answers with the expected and immediate, "No." But another clap of thunder causes him to change his mind. "Yes." Iron-Man is dropped to the floor.

The four of them go outside into the early darkness. They sit on the wicker seat, watching the black and livid storm together. Low clouds pass in dreary cadence across the shadowed sky, hovering over the earth like a visiting creature with massive power and breadth as its black belly drops down heavy rain. Bright flashes of lighting cut through the sky as the showers are thrown to the ground in waves. The wind pushes, rips, and pulls at trees and everything that will move, causing the rain to course down at an angle as it pushes the clouds steadily on. Blooms from flowering trees skitter through the air, floating up and away in the torrent. Mist dashes up from the porch's edge and the railing, touching the family's skin with a continuous spray that is cool and strangely gentle. Jeremiah is thankful for the storm as it draws his children into his arms in captivation.

Lightning dashes through the sky in a jagged bolt, brightening homes and trees in a flash. Gavin holds his face in a wince of expectation, and Jeremiah hugs Abigail firmly. The expected crack comes like war and Abigail calls out in startle, "Oooooooh!" Cole's eyes are blue and wide as he takes in the storm. He announces, "That thunder was super duper duper duper duper big!" his arms stretched out from his body.

Jeremiah agrees, "It was." Lightning flashes, brightening in an instant and gone again. Jeremiah cautions, "This is going to be a big one."

The warning takes away the sharpness, and the father with his children remain quiet as it cracks out. The four continue to watch. Awe sits with them. Jeremiah's hair grows wet with the accumulation of mist, causing a drop to drip from his dark hair and down onto Abigail, her light-brown hair absorbing it.

The screen door opens. Bri pokes her head out. "Enjoying the storm?" she asks.

Gavin mouths through his blanket, "Yeah."

Cole exclaims, "Momma, there was lightning and it was super duper duper loud!"

She smiles. "I heard it."

Gavin asks, "Mom, can I come back inside?"

"Sure." Bri keeps the door open.

Gavin hops down. Jeremiah says, "I thought you were having fun out here with me."

"I was. But now I want to go inside."

"Okay," Jeremiah says, glad that Gavin at least admitted his enjoyment. Abigail leans over Jeremiah's shoulder, reaching for Bri as well. Jeremiah knows the moment is over. He offers his baby girl to Bri, stretching her out towards his wife. Abigail kicks her little legs in the air like a frog as she lurches her way closer until finally in her mother's arms.

Bri sweeps Abigail to her shoulder and says, "Dinner will be ready shortly," and returns inside.

Alone with Cole, Jeremiah attempts to scoop his son up, but Cole squirms against his father and says, "Papa, I don't want to sit on your lap!"

"Oh, okay," Jeremiah feigns agreement.

Cole announces again, "I don't want to sit on your lap!"

Jeremiah releases Cole and places him by his side again, content to at least have his boy next to him – his boy whose independence is quickly outgrowing his size. He places his arm around his son, but Cole calls out again, "Papa!"

"Sheesh, Cole! Okay!" Jeremiah's arm retreats.

Stan's white work van drives by, parking at the top of his driveway. The storm assaults Stan as he clambers out through the driver's side door. With shoulders hunched, he jogs across the cul-de-sac through the rain and puddles with his chin down and a hand to his brow to keep the droplets from his eyes. He huffs a moment on the top step of Jeremiah's porch, propped up on the white railing as he bends in. His head sticks out from his scrawny neck, looking like a turtle that may have lost its shell.

Jeremiah offers, "Hey, Stan, wrong house, bud."

"Oh, I know," Stan responds with southern courtesy. "I'm sorry to trouble you, I know it's been a long day, I'm sure. Working and all."

"Sure, what's up?" Jeremiah pushes along.

"Just wondering about the jar. Hope it's not too much of an interruption."

"The jar?" Jeremiah's dark eyes hide his amusement.

"Yes, sir, that jar your wife brought over for me to open. I couldn't do it, and I just wanted to know if you had had a chance to try it out, is all."

His eyes back on the storm, wet hair dangling down, Jeremiah comments, "You walked through this storm after a long day of work to ask about that jar?"

Stan shows no shame. "Yes, sir, I did."

Jeremiah announces, "I opened it." The fabled conqueror of jars.

"How long did it take?" Stan can't contain himself.

"No time at all. I just grabbed it and turned it open."

Stan taps his foot up and down, contemplating, and says simply, "Hmmmm, that's something," considering the possibility of having caught Jeremiah in a straight-out Yankee lie.

Jeremiah offers, "I'm sure you loosened it up for me."

"Yeah, I was thinking that very same thing," Stan states.

Cole's smart eyes, round and inquisitive, take Stan in as his little mind has picked up details, and the boy concludes, "You are strong. But Papa is super duper strong."

Stan nods, unoffended. "That he sure is. Well, good night y'all." He turns and runs back through the storm to his home.

Jeremiah lays his arm over Cole, this time permitted by his son to rest it there. They watch the storm together until called in for dinner.

5

Cole stares out of the car window as Jeremiah drives them home. They travel the winding street laid long between the trees. Dense and dark gray clouds are above. Rain falling. In his car seat, Cole is steadily hypnotized by the dull drumming on the windshield and the rhythmic sliding of the wipers. His eyes are glassy. The vanilla Frosty Cole has been enjoying has melted down his arm, white ice cream trickling down his sleeve in streams and to the floor as it drips from points of accumulation. He grips the soggy cone, as if there might still be something salvageable, or he simply forgot about it being there.

Cole's eyes blink, holding a moment before opening again, and he asks, "Papa, are we almost home?"

"Soon, bud. Soon. Don't fall asleep, okay?"

"Okay." Cole straightens in his seat and the small boy widens his eyes in an act of resolve to stay awake. But his eyes soon grow heavy again. Cole blinks and nods, his head shooting upright here and there as the transition of sleep and wake tosses him. The ice cream cone tilts downward.

Jeremiah orients the rearview mirror to provide him a view of his son. Cole notices, his eyes turning tiredly to the mirror. He says in a partial whisper, "Papa, don't look at me."

In an attempt to keep the mood light and his son engaged, Jeremiah assures, "I'm not looking at you. I'm looking at your head."

Appeased, Cole says, "Okay." He then returns his gaze to the rain and the trees, as though they might be speaking quiet wonders to him. His eyes blink again.

The windshield wipers fly back and forth. The rain now douses the windshield in buckets, coursing down in a blinding storm. It pounds loudly atop the roof in tin-tin thuds as though wanting to pierce through to get inside. Jeremiah focuses on the white line at the road's edge for a guide as he's forced to stay more alert. Puddles cause the wheels to hydroplane until hitting asphalt again. Jeremiah considers pulling over to wait for the storm to pass, he can barely see, but the desire to just be home and get Cole in bed keeps him going.

"Papa, why are those lights doing that?"

Jeremiah, so focused on the line of the road, hadn't even noticed the path ahead. "Those are called *hazard lights*."

"What's that?"

"It lets other cars know that they need help or to watch out for them."

"Oh."

Jeremiah slows as they draw near the small white car pulled over. It sits parked on the gravel, stopped between the road and the edge of an aged pond with tall grass and cattails, hazard lights blinking drearily. Clearing to the side of the tinkered car, Jeremiah sees no one inside and assumes the people ran out of gas or some other trouble sat them there. He can't help but be thankful it wasn't them.

They continue further ahead. Cole says, "Look at those people."

Through a squint, Jeremiah states, "I see them."

Like ghosts appearing, two people walk together at the edge of the road. The rain assaults their cowered heads, their clothes plastered along their limbs. Coming nearer, Jeremiah sees that the taller of the two is a woman, her grayish hair drenched and matted along her back, her dress soaked and sagging on her like a hindrance. The boy to her right trudges, dragging his steps. Mud drips from their feet. Water hangs from them. Jeremiah begins to speed up, as though he never noticed them. He doesn't want to meet the their pleading gazes.

"Papa, are you going to help them?"

The thought hadn't even crossed Jeremiah's mind. "I don't think so."

"Papa, they're super-duper wet."

"I know. But I want to get you home to bed."

"Papa, the good guy picked up the hurt guy who was beat up by bad guys."

"What?" Jeremiah stifles a simmering irritation. He then realizes, "Are you talking about the good Samaritan?"

Cole answers in tired tones, "No, I'm talking about the good guy who picked up the hurt guy who was beat up by bad guys. He had a donkey."

"Right. Did you learn about that in Sunday school?"

"Yes."

"It's the story of the *Good Samaritan.*'

"No it's not," Cole answers, and rather than enter into an argument, Jeremiah lets it go. Cole says again, "They're super duper wet."

"Great." Jeremiah sighs as the words of his son pick at his conscience. If he is going to change, if he is going to be more positive, then this would be a good test of such resolve. As he pulls the car over onto the rocky shoulder, just ahead of the two people, Jeremiah turns around with his right arm strung atop the passenger seat as he charges his son with, "Cole, one of them is going to have to sit next to you. I don't want you talking to them."

"Why not?"

"I just don't want you to." Jeremiah's eyes are serious as he wishes he didn't have to explain such things, as he wishes the earth and her children could be trusted.

"But why?"

Jeremiah knows he's being overcautious, but the old adage still finds it's way out of his own lips, "Better safe than sorry."

The woman and the boy jog their way up to the car with smiles of relief showing through the ceaseless downpour. The unlock button clicks as Jeremiah times it with their nearness so they can know they're welcomed inside. The car doors shut with soggy clicks as the two of them drop down into the car seats, the woman in front and the boy in back. They swipe at drippings. The woman tosses wet dangles of stringy hair from her face. The boy wipes his face with a soaked sleeve.

"Thank you," the woman says. "Thank you!"

The boy lets out a simple, "Wow, that storm is big!"

The stench of them is awful. Their stink fills the car as if instantly possessing it as their own, the smell of body odor and unwashed clothes, wet dog and soiled sheets and canned beans. Jeremiah almost gags at the thick stench as it climbs his nostrils. Quickly, Jeremiah reminds himself not to judge, to not allow the plank in his eye to cause him to go blind, remembering that by entertaining strangers some have unwittingly entertained angels. Water finds its way onto his pants and sleeve in large drops as Jeremiah lowers his window to allow the slim opening to thin out the stench.

"God bless you! God bless you!" The woman consecrates Jeremiah and the car with her thankfulness. She's grateful from head to toe, her teeth gleaming within her upstretched smile. Her fingers are bony, and her forearms frail. A tarnished golden cross dangles between her shriveled breasts. She rubs her hands together as though trying to warm them from a chill and she introduces, "I'm Geraldine."

"I'm Jeremiah."

"You smell bad!" Cole announces.

Jeremiah cringes at the honest comment from his son. But the two of them, woman and boy, chuckle without offense, as if maybe they're from a different country where such things are common and preferred, and the young child simply doesn't understand their ways.

"Sorry," Jeremiah offers.

"No, no, no," Geraldine assures with a wag of her hand.

As he pulls back out onto the road, Jeremiah looks over his left shoulder, hitting the gas to make sure there isn't a traveling car hidden in the storm that will rear-end them. The pale, stringy muscles of Geraldine's neck stretch taut as she turns to watch her own car and the pond shrink behind them. She announces, "We were on the way to the gas station to fill up, but well, we didn't make it." She laughs as if it were a common punch line to a well-known joke. "We started to walk, but that storm came on us something awful."

Jeremiah agrees, recalling the rains of the past weeks, not a dry day in the whole month of April. "I know. This whole spring has been full of rain. The other day I was mowing – bright out and all – next thing I know I'm having to run back into the house because of a downpour."

Geraldine nods wholeheartedly, as if remembering that very moment.

"Well, you're a handsome boy!" Geraldine announces as she looks over her seat at Cole, her fingers at the seat's corner as she orients herself to him as best she can. There's youth in her hazel eyes and sweetness in her voice, like honeysuckle.

Cole states, "Girls are pretty. Boys are handsome."

"That's right," she agrees, then compliments him again, like handing out lollipops at the dentist office, "and you're very smart. I can see that, for sure."

"Where can I take you?" Jeremiah asks.

"There's a little gas station up about three miles from here."

"Off Mitchel Mill," Jeremiah says, almost to himself. Tilting the rearview mirror, he gets a view of the boy. There's a splinter of space between Cole and him. "What's your name?" Jeremiah asks.

The boy sits up and answers, "Mike."

"It's good to meet you, Mike."

"Good meet you too, sir." The boy's manners are courteous and respectful. His frame is strong and healthy at the shoulders, as though he lives on a farm. He has the same hazel eyes as his mother.

"What grade are you in?" Jeremiah asks as he slows at a green light, wanting to ensure no one is coming through at the cross section.

"Seventh."

"You like school?"

"Yes, sir, I do."

"That's good. What's your favorite class?"

Mike answers, "Curriculum Assistance."

"What's that?" Jeremiah asks. "I never had a class like that, but it's been years since I was in school." He chuckles at his age.

Geraldine answers, "It's for children who have an IEP. Mike is a little slow."

"Oh, sorry." Jeremiah apologizes.

"No worries, no worries. You didn't know."

Mike asks of Cole, "What's your name?" Jeremiah watches in the mirror. His guard is coming down as the reality of their genuine plight dispels his easy paranoia. These are good people and he's glad to be helping them. He appreciates the challenge by his son to do the Christian thing, and he wonders how many more lessons he has in store, where his children will teach him more than he ever teaches them.

Cole answers, "I'm Cole. But Gavin calls me, 'Cole-zilla,' because I destroy his toys."

Geraldine and Mike laugh at this, Geraldine first as Mike catches on to the cuteness of the boy and how much he just said in such a small telling.

Geraldine stretches forward, pointing through the windshield. "Just up there on the right."

"Okay," Jeremiah answers. He's passed the gas station a few times before, but never stopped because he always assumed the pumps had no credit card swipe, the sort of gas station where elderly men sit out front in wooden chairs and offer their aged critiques on fancy things like cars and phones and other thing-a-ma-jigs that make life go too fast. He pulls near to the closed garage doors.

Geraldine announces, "Good, Madge is here. She can drive us back."

Jeremiah offers, "Are you sure? I can wait and take you back to your car." He wants to go the full way. Go two miles when asked to go one.

"No, no, no, you've helped us plenty, and we sure are grateful. Saved us the brunt of the storm and a lot of walking too. My old bones would have been strung up sore for days if we walked all that. I hope we can repay the kind act one day." She shuts the door without a chance for further courtesy from Jeremiah. "C'mon, Mike," she calls.

Mike thanks them both. He then offers, "Good to meet you, Cole," as though wanting to make sure the small boy feels like he was a part of the adult world for short while.

"Yep," Cole responds. The door is shut closed. Geraldine waves to another aged lady standing by the repair center where large signs for Inspection and Oil Change hang. Geraldine calls out loudly through the waning storm, "Madge!"

The woman named Madge tucks Geraldine and Mike beneath her umbrella, walking them back to the shop. The bells above the store's entrance jingle as they go inside.

Jeremiah puts his car in gear. He asks, "Ready to go home, Cole?" But the young boy is already asleep, his body slumped and his head resting against the cushion. His arms draped over his thighs. Ice cream on the floor. He breathes deep in quiet dreams.

Jeremiah smiles at his son through the mirror yet again. "Okay, sweet boy. Let's get home and put you to bed."

6

Golden beams glow in a cascading haze across the floor and table, reaching to Jeremiah at the counter. He does dishes at the sink in the quiet kitchen. Music plays from small speakers, barely heard in somber melody of piano and violin.

Bri comes into the kitchen, Abigail in her arms. With his hands in the scalding water and suds, Jeremiah turns and smiles. Bri smiles too. She says on behalf of her daughter, "Good morning, Papa,"

"Good morning," Jeremiah replies in a whisper.

The baby girl's bright eyes brighten at the site of her father. Jeremiah tosses water from his hands with a few shakes before reaching for her. Abigail stretches from her mother and towards Jeremiah, arms outstretched as she bobs up and down. Jeremiah takes and holds her. From over her father's shoulder, Abigail begins pointing at a picture on the wall, wanting Jeremiah to name the people and tell her stories like he does. Her eyes are focused, clear and wide as they remain intent on a family photo taken when she was a newborn. Jeremiah leans towards his wife for a kiss and then asks, "Ready for coffee?"

"Yes," Bri answers. She says again, "Yes."

"Okay, take Abigail back for a minute."

Bri says, "Just put her in the living room." As Jeremiah takes a few steps out of the kitchen, Bri instructs, "And make sure there are no Angry Birds on the floor."

"Sure."

Jeremiah sets Abigail down onto the carpet, but the baby girl whimpers as she sits and looks up at him pleadingly. She reaches for him again, almost tumbling forward.

Kneeling low to place himself near his daughter, Jeremiah comforts Abigail with a hand along her neck as he rests kisses on her forehead and cheek. He offers her soft assurances, "I'll hold you in a minute. I need to make coffee for Momma or she won't be very happy." Jeremiah provides Abigail a red Angry Bird which she secures tight in a fist. Abigail looks at Jeremiah a moment to see what he'll do. He smiles with a nod of permission, and she plops the Angry Bird into her mouth. Her cheek bulges. She crawls away.

"Time to make the donuts," Jeremiah says as he stands.

"Donuts!" Cole yells from the steps.

Not knowing Cole was there, Jeremiah explains, "Oops, no, sorry. It's just a saying."

"We're having donuts!" Cole claps with enthusiasm as he yells up to Gavin behind him.

Stepping to the bottom step in dragging slippers, Gavin asks, "We're having donuts?" His own eyes brighten, as if the reality of donuts might be the answer to most of life's answers, but no one ever dared to accept the simplicity.

"It's a saying," Jeremiah states again, feeling old, feeling the possible beginning of such phrases as *back in my day* and *kids these days* and *yappidy yappidy yappidy*. He explains, "*Time to make the donuts* was from a commercial for Dunkin' Donuts. The guy, whatever his name was, would be tired and hit his alarm clock and say, 'Time to make the donuts,' and then go and make them. He was tired. And I'm tired. So it makes sense." Vacant eyes stare up at him. Jeremiah declares, "Yep, it was pretty awesome."

He goes into the kitchen and grabs up his keys while he announces, "Let's go get donuts."

"Yay!" the brothers celebrate,

Jeremiah apologizes to his wife, "I'll make coffee when I get back."

"You better."

They drive to the nearby store. Jeremiah blinks often. Eyes tired. From the backseat, Gavin asks, "Papa?"

"Yeah?"

"Why do we call Uncle Langdon, Uncle Langdon?"

Jeremiah asks, "What else would we call him?"

Cole states, "Uncle Langdon is our Uncle."

"Exactly," Jeremiah says with a grin.

Gavin says, "But you don't have any brothers or sisters."

"You're right."

"So why do we call Uncle Langdon, Uncle Langdon?"

Cole says again, "Uncle Langdon is our Uncle."

Jeremiah glances at Gavin through the rearview mirror. He says, "Your Uncle Langdon is very close to me. I've known him for years and he's the best friend I've ever had. He's like a brother to me. So, when Mommy was pregnant with you, I knew Langdon would be your uncle."

"Oh." Gavin then asks, "Because you and Uncle Langdon are kind of like me and Cole?"

"Exactly."

Gavin asks, "Does Uncle Langdon have brothers?"

"Yep."

"Does he have sisters?"

"No."

"Oh."

Jeremiah says, "Your Uncle Langdon is very close to his brothers. He talks about them all the time."

"What are they like?"

"I don't know."

"Why not?"

"I've never met them. They don't live near here."

Gavin asks, "Where do they live?"

"In Chicago."

"Where's that?"

"It's in a different country that's really cold and ugly."

"Oh. I don't want to go there."

"Just kidding. It's in America."

Cole says, "America is the United States."

Jeremiah says, "That's right."

Gavin asks, "When Uncle Langdon has kids, will they call you Uncle Papa? Or maybe Uncle Jeremiah?"

"I'm not sure. I guess that's up to your Uncle Langdon. They definitely won't call me Uncle Papa."

Cole states, "You're Papa and You're Jeremiah."

"Well, I'm your Papa. To everyone else, I'm just Jeremiah or knucklehead."

"What's a knucklehead?"

"Just kidding. I'm just being stupid. I'm very tired."

"Oh. Why are you tired?" Gavin asks.

"I was up early."

"Why?"

"I don't know. I just was."

"Oh." Gavin asks, "Can we get two donuts?"

Jeremiah answers, "Not a chance."

"Why not?"

"'Cause you'll go bonkers."

"Why will we go bonkers?"

"It'd be way too much sugar for you to handle."

"Maybe when I'm big I'll buy two donuts," Gavin says.

"Yep, when you're big, you can buy as many donuts as you want. One time, I ate twelve donuts. I almost got sick."

Gavin's eyes widen in amazement at his father's proclamation of such a mythical feat. "Twelve donuts!" he says.

"Yep. It was terrible. But delicious, too."

"When I get big, I'll eat twelve donuts," Gavin says with a smile, as though he just realized with clarity what he wants to be when he grows up.

"I'll buy three donuts," Cole says, "because I'm three years old."

"That sounds good too," says Jeremiah.

They park at a local store, the parking lot nearly empty. Jeremiah unbuckles and says, "Alright, boys. Time to get donuts so that we can get back and make coffee for Mommy."

Cole states, "And then you'll go to work."

"Yep. And then I'll go to work."

Jeremiah walks between his sons, holding a hand in each of his.

7

"Because I need to do an oil-change. No, I didn't pick up dinner for the whole family. Yes. I just got something for me and Cole. I'm sorry. Jeez. No. I guess I wasn't thinking. I just wanted to spend some time with my son. I haven't seen him much lately. Is that so bad? Would you stop? That's enough. I'll be home soon. I'm just getting oil change stuff. I already said that. Good-bye." Jeremiah hangs up, purposefully withholding the usual "I love you," with hopes his wife will notice and be hurt.

"Keep walking, Cole, I need to get some things for an oil change," Jeremiah says as they move deeper into Wal-Mart, his words and feet pushed on by a mixture of exhaustion and irritability. He can feel harshness building within, tension coursing down his arms, exercising his fingers.

Cole's little body wobbles drowsily as he shuffles beside his father. He fusses, "I want to go look at the toys."

"Keep walking. It won't be much longer. Then we'll go home." Jeremiah can hear the approach of a thunderstorm. He states in aggravation, "It's going to rain again." He can't help the complaint.

Jeremiah places his hand at the back of Cole's shoulder and presses the boy further forward, urging him to keep a good pace. Cole plops to the ground to avoid his father and begins crying in frustration on the floor. This isn't like Cole, but despite this, it inspires no sympathy from Jeremiah who says through gritted teeth, "Get up."

People move past the two of them, some stopping momentarily as if eyeing a car accident along the side of the road. Feeling their eyes, Jeremiah reaches down and snags Cole by his arm, pulling him to his feet. Cole stands, a fist at his eye to rub the tears away.

Jeremiah picks his son up, crossing his arms beneath Cole's bottom to hold him to his chest. In a controlled tone that hides his aggravation, Jeremiah concedes, "Do you want to come with me, or do you want to look at the toys?" He attempts to sound understanding. His moods have returned the past few days, overflowing, and his children and wife have suffered his harsher tones. He has to try harder. He has to remember. He looks at his boy, eyes loving and patient. Cole smiles and hugs his father and rests his head on his father's shoulder. It soothes Jeremiah.

Cole answers, "I want to look at toys. Then you can pick me up again."

"Okay." Jeremiah escorts Cole to the aisle of toys. The high shelves hold boxes of potential action and color and various figures for play with smiles and excitement to offer. Cole's eyes gaze up and down. Pulling his son's attention, Jeremiah instructs, "Cole, listen, I'm going right over there to get some oil. I'll just be a few aisles away. You stay here. I'll be right back." He pulls Cole into a hug. "I'm sorry for being so mean sometimes."

"It's okay, Papa."

Jeremiah says, "No, it's not."

"Okay."

"Okay?" Jeremiah smiles.

"Okay." Cole rests his body against his father's chest. Jeremiah again reconsiders just carrying his son, but he knows it would be much quicker if he can move alone. Time is drawing on longer than he wanted. He should have been home an hour ago. He needs to get home so he can apologize to Bri as well. Besides, he already promised Cole that he could look at the toys.

"I'll be right back."

"Okay, Papa."

Cole turns towards a row of toys and picks up a box of Star Wars Angry Birds. Jeremiah's fingers drift from his son as he moves past. Walking hurriedly, Jeremiah brushes past people and displays, continuing along in a determined pace. At the automotive section, he drops down, knowing precisely where the Fram #4967 oil filter is located. He reaches for it, but the one he's looking for isn't there. He grits his teeth. "Of course." He pushes numbered boxes aside and peers into the back of the shelves. He shuffles a few steps to the left as he stays crouched and performs the same search, scanning over numbers and sizes, in anger knocking over the ones he doesn't need. His phone rings in his pocket. He draws it out. It's Bri. He considers answering. It rings again. But he drops it back into his pocket with the ringer on silent. A few more filters are knocked to the floor and he leaves them there. Finally, he finds the one he wants placed in a completely different section. "Of course."

Jeremiah grips the oil jug in his left hand while pinching the filter between his bicep and ribs in preparation for scooping Cole up and carrying him in his right arm. He heads back for his son.

"Time to go, bud," Jeremiah announces as he turns the corner of the aisle, sounding successful and less tense as he's closer to being home.

An empty aisle.

Jeremiah closes his eyes. "Cole, I told you not to move."

Jeremiah walks the length of the aisle. He circles displays of stacked toys, expecting the small figure of his son to meet him. He goes through the aisle of board games on the other side, then walks down each toy aisle again. Scanning left to right and back again, Cole is not in sight, despite Jeremiah's mind creating such an expectation. He returns to where he began. Jeremiah places the oil and filter on a random shelf.

"Cole!" he calls out, his voice reaching over the high displays.

As he continues back through the aisles, Jeremiah can almost see himself and Cole missing each other like some comedy routine from generations ago, Cole down one aisle peeking for his father, while Jeremiah peeks at the other end, missing each other each time.

Jeremiah calls out, "Cole!" He can hear his own growing desperation.

Children have congregated at the same area of Angry Birds, they look to be about Gavin's age. Jeremiah jogs up to them and asks, "Have you seen a small boy? He has short dirty-blond hair, and he was wearing a Spider-Man shirt and red rain boots. He has blue eyes."

The three children look up at him in blank unresponsiveness and Jeremiah asks harshly, "Have you seen him?"

The tallest answers, "No." And the kids return their attention to the toys.

Jeremiah turns back around and decides to go to the automotive section he was at moments ago – Cole must have gone there for him. Jeremiah looks over each face he passes and searches every space between as he dashes to the auto section where two old men debate about a thing.

Cole isn't there.

Jeremiah interrupts their conversation. "Have you seen a small boy?"

They turn towards him. "What's that?"

"Have you seen a small boy?"

The old men look at each other, as though to gauge their answer, and then turn back with one of them answering, "Nope. No, sir."

Jeremiah travels random areas. His brain scans through countless possibilities as he tries to decide what the best option might be to cover space in this store and find his son. Wal-Mart is now a monstrous maze expanding every second with countless paths and hiding places as the continuous image of Cole in red rain boots searching for his father plays out in Jeremiah's mind. He imagines Cole crying. Jeremiah runs.

He moves past people, grabbing shoulders and pushing through as he asks in begging anguish, "Have you seen a small boy?" Blank faces of confusion. False concern.

"Cole!" A few more steps, "Cole! Cole!"

He goes to the children's clothes. Cole must be looking at T-shirts with superheroes.

"Cole!"

Back to the toys. One more time.

"Cole!"

The auto section.

"Cole!"

Jeremiah runs to the customer service desk. There's a line of only a few people. He stands at the back, sweating and breathing heavily as he continues to search for his son. He imagines Cole in each check-out line, along each square on the floor, behind each cart, then gone again.

"And what I don't like is that you told me I could bring this back and now you're saying I can't!" An obese woman argues with the customer service attendant, her body flapping and shaking as she demands an answer.

The cashier explains, "Ma'am, I never told you that. It's against policy to return video games or movies that have been opened."

"Yes, you did! Oh, yes, you did! That is a bold face lie! You stood right there and told me I could bring this back if I didn't like it!"

"Ma'am, that's completely against policy. It is something I would not tell anyone. Now, I'm sorry if you misunderstood me."

"So, now you're saying I'm dumb! Now you're saying I'm stupid! I guess I can't even understand English!" The heavyset woman turns to the people behind her as though she might rile up support.

Jeremiah murmurs, "There's no time for this." He skims the edge of the line as he moves to the front. Placing his hands on the counter to earn an attentive ear, he states clearly, clean, loud, "My son is missing."

The wide woman declares with her face stretched toward him, "You can't cut me!"

The cashier too ignores Jeremiah as she steadies her attention onto the woman, stating plainly, "Sir, I'll help you as soon as I can. One at a time."

"My son is missing," Jeremiah says again, his heart pounding with panic at the repeated announcement. "My son is missing. I need to find him."

"He's by the toys, I can tell you that!" The breasts of the woman bounce with the effort of her assertion. The woman's finger points just inches from Jeremiah, causing his hand to twitch, wanting to snap her finger in half.

He turns his attention back to the cashier as he attempts again, "Please, I can't find my son. He was over at the toys and I looked all over and I can't find him. He's only three. He's wearing a Spider man shirt and some rain boots. Red rain boots. He has short dirty blond hair and blue eyes. His name is Cole."

"Sir, I'll be right with you and we'll find your son. Just a minute more, that's all. I'm sure he's somewhere by the toys."

Jeremiah shouts, "My son doesn't have a minute!" He's unable to believe the people around him, these people with skin and faces. "Call your manager now and help me find my son!" He then begs, "Please, for my son, call someone who can help me."

The cashier does, lifting the phone. The large woman pushes her way into Jeremiah's face, telling him to be careful because he doesn't know her, doesn't know what she would do to him if he were in her neighborhood and he better watch himself. Jeremiah turns his shoulder.

A manager comes up slowly, lack of care for much of anything is in his fatigued face of unaccomplished tasks. He asks questions and explains options and asks questions. Twenty minutes later, security calls are going out through the intercom to anyone who might hear. Four associates help by searching throughout the store, while Jeremiah runs corner to corner and back again between with loud calls of, "Cole!" Running endlessly. Calling every few steps. "Cole!"

An hour goes by. Security guards shake their heads talking about reports and other actions they can take now that they're certain Cole isn't in the store. They check the video. Nothing much because things weren't how they were supposed to be. The police are contacted.

The phone is at Jeremiah's ear. Bri asks questions on the other end. She's upset. She's angry at him for being thoughtless. He's been letting his moods control him again. Jeremiah listens. Numbed and listless. When Bri is done, he says, "Cole is missing. I can't find him. Cole is gone, and I don't know where he is."

He hangs up with nothing left to say.

Jeremiah stands alone. The busyness of the store continues to toss and shuffle around him. In his empty hand, Jeremiah can feel the absence of small fingers. Can still feel the warmth of his son against his chest. Tears form in his eyes. He starts to sob, hands to his face.

At Jeremiah's feet, a flowing forms. Something like water. The beginning of waves tossing at his toes, small waves made of fear and anger, feeding on the same and rising quickly as Jeremiah stands in the missing of his son.

Part Two

8

The ceiling fan spins above as Jeremiah stands in the center of the living room. His body wobbles faintly. Gavin rests against his father's leg, his arms secured around Jeremiah's thigh. Jeremiah places a hand absently on top of his son's head. Bri weeps on the couch. Abigail plays on the ground, crawling from toy to toy.

The police officer stands near the door and asks questions, his hat pinched at the bend in his arm. He uses a thumb to flip a page in his little notebook, scribbling details as Jeremiah explains what happened and anything else that may be helpful in the search for Cole. Jeremiah's plastic lips move with answers. At times he's barely audible.

The notebook is slapped shut and dropped into the officer's pocket. Black hat returned to his head. The policeman offers assurance that the department will do everything they can to find Cole and he explains that it might be good for the family to "put boots to the pavement" by placing fliers and organizing friends and family to help in finding Cole. He says, "He'll be back," as though it was a misunderstanding. A casual trouble.

The officer encourages, "Keep your spirits up. We'll find him." He leaves the home.

The hum of the fan drones on. Bri sobs between her fingers. Abigail plays. Gavin stands at his father's side. Jeremiah stares blankly at the closed door.

9

"We're not sure where Cole is," Bri attempts to explain.

"But when will he be back?" Gavin asks.

"I don't know. Soon."

"But where did he go?"

"We don't know."

"Are the police going to find him?"

"They will." Bri rocks Gavin back and forth as he sits on her lap.

"Okay, good. I want to see him."

Jeremiah comes downstairs, holding a stack of papers. He passes by Bri and Gavin and goes into the kitchen. The faucet is turned on. He drinks water. A granola bar is crunched down. Wrapper dropped into the trash. At the front door, Jeremiah slides boots on. Bends to tie them.

Bri asks, "Do you want to eat something before you go?"

"No. I ate."

"A granola bar isn't enough, hon'."

"It's plenty. I have to go."

"Are you planning on being out long again?"

"As long as I need to. At least until all the fliers are up. I plan on going to the mall to talk to people, too."

"You should eat something."

"I already told you, I did."

Gavin sits up. "Where are you going, Papa?"

"To find Cole."

Gavin says, "Oh." He then asks, "Can I go with you?"

Jeremiah slings on a gray hoodie. "No, sorry." The door closes.

Gavin asks, "Why can't I go with Papa?"

Bri answers, "Papa has a lot of places he needs to go and he just wants to go fast so he can get it done as quick as he can."

"So he can find Cole quicker?"

"Yes."

"Okay, good. I miss him. I hope Papa finds Cole tonight."

Bri whimpers. "Me too."

Bri rests back against the cushions and pulls her son to her chest, stroking Gavin's hair and coaxing him to comfort as she prays and prays for her baby boy to come home soon.

10

"Anything? You've got to be kidding me. How many officers do you have looking? Is anyone looking?" On the phone, Jeremiah questions the detective assigned to their case. He paces from kitchen to living room to dining room to kitchen and back again in circling laps. "Well, what are you doing? There's got to be more you can do. What do I *want* you to do? Everything you can! I highly doubt that. It sounds like you're doing nothing. Well, you're not doing everything you can, that's for sure. Yes, I've been putting up fliers. Yes, I've been putting them everywhere I can. The best thing to do is wait? Is that a joke? Wait for what? Wait for my son to just walk through the door *'oh, hey, Papa I'm back.'* Is that it? Maybe wait for whoever took him to just bring him home, *'Sorry, didn't realize this wasn't my boy.'* You have to go? That's funny. That's right, you do need to go, you need to go find my son. You need to do *that!* Okay, fine. Yeah, sorry for bothering you. Call me if you hear anything, you know, if you end up doing your job."

Jeremiah shoves the phone into his pocket in an act of anger. He snags up the stack of fliers piled atop the counter and heads to the front door. Looking up from the laptop, Bri stops Jeremiah with her words as she announces, "I've been posting as much as I can online."

"Okay, good. Anything?" He wishes he hadn't asked.

"No, not yet. But a lot of people are messaging us, telling us they're praying and trying to offer encouragement."

"Well, that's great. Do we have a lot of thumb up *likes*?" He can't help himself.

Bri begs, "Don't, Jeremiah."

"I know. I'm sorry. I'm going out to put up more fliers and ask around at all the local stores."

"Okay good. You've been gone all the time lately. Are you sure you don't want to eat with us tonight? Even just for a minute, just so Gavin and Abigail can see you?"

"No. I need to go."

"Okay. I love you." Bri goes to rise so she can offer her husband a kiss and a hug, but the door is shut before she stands. The car drives away. Bri hears Abigail awake from her nap, talking in her crib. She goes to care for the small girl.

11

Jeremiah lies in bed staring at the ceiling. He watches the fan spin in the dark empty night. The streetlamp at the curve of the cul-de-sac ushers pale light through the window, showing in abstraction the furniture of the room and the pile of clothes dropped on the floor by Jeremiah day after day. He can feel the hatred and fear stir around within him. He can hear his wife's pained breathing.

Bri turns over. She wraps her leg and arm around her husband. She draws her body close to his and buries her face into his neck. She sobs, scattering the quiet with her tears.

The shroud of self-hatred Jeremiah has covered himself with begins to thin, melted by his wife's sadness and the warmth of her body. Jeremiah folds himself into the arms of his wife and holds her tightly, sobbing with her.

12

The sun sets colorless beneath the expanse of outstretched rainclouds as they blacken into darker shades with the disappearance of another day. Bruised vestiges of purple touch the end of the horizon as the only evidence of the sun's departure. From the wicker seat, Jeremiah stares out from the front porch. He looks over the familiar houses of neighbors before him and can see glimpses of the neighborhood beyond. Everything earns his mistrust. All of creation has been tainted before his bloodshot eyes, sleepless and tortured. Every shadow hides his son. Every door.

Afar off past the trees, his mind's eye carries Jeremiah over an endless earth that has opened its mouth and swallowed his son. He feels like a prisoner isolated away in a concrete tower, permitted only to watch the sun come and go as the rest of the world moves about in their freedoms. Jeremiah asks desperately of the deaf and coming night, "Where would I hide a child?"

The answer is there. Behind his ears. But saying it out loud instills a seed of hopelessness inside of Jeremiah, bound to sprout and bloom.

A voice answers. His own. "In my own home."

The uttered confession disturbs a panic within Jeremiah's chest, tightening it in asphyxiation. He gasps. He can't catch his breath. He gasps again, sucking at air. An attempt to regain his breath. Hand to his chest. He stands to find air and breathes a little easier. Just barely.

His eyes fill with tears. Jeremiah shakes the railing in a fit of futile frustration as he begs through gritted teeth, "Please. I just want my son."

Part Three

13

Running. Running as fast as he can. Arms pumping. Feet dashing. Lungs stretched and screaming. Aisles fly by. More and more. He stops, digging his heels into the linoleum, and he looks, thinking maybe he missed a glance of his baby boy. A flash of a pant leg. A corner of boot. A toss of hair. Glances of Cole are everywhere. But never the whole of his son. Jeremiah hesitates in the height and breadth of the store, turning in all directions.

"Cole!"

He's running again.

"Cole!"

Jeremiah's shoes slam out in heavy reverberations as he yells through the empty forsaken store, "Cole! Where are you? Please come back! Please! I'm right here! Come to my voice! Cole!"

His words echo back, like the call of mockers, displaying back to Jeremiah his futility in fainter tones that fade smaller and smaller until gone. He's running. Running again because he doesn't know what else to do. And he's crying. Crying because he knows. What does he know?

Jeremiah is startled awake. His wife's hand is at his shoulder, shaking him. He blinks in confusion as he finds himself back in his bedroom where the muted hues of blackness hide the terror on his face.

"Jeremiah." Bri sounds afraid. Concerned.

"What?" His voice is coarse and ragged.

Bri is only an outline in the darkness, but her tone tells the worry she feels. "You were," she pauses, "crying."

"Oh," he states. His shirt is soaked, sagging with sweat from his body as he sits up. Feet off the end of the bed, Jeremiah's flesh trembles a moment.

"Where are you going?" Bri asks from the sheets.

"To head back out."

"You just laid down a couple of hours ago. You haven't slept in days."

"So?" He stands from the bed and leaves.

14

He staples the flier to the street post. Four metal clicks. He jogs to the next post and does the same, staying in the sun and the oppressive heat. The asphalt resonates in pulsing waves that rise and cook the air. His neck and forearms are scorched. He's tired and thirsty. He licks at chapped lips. He nears the next post. The staple gun clicks empty as he attempts to use it, and he curses at it before smashing it against the post. Refilling the slot, he slams it shut and finishes the flier and runs ahead to the next post.

He's been working through the entirety of the neighborhood, his backpack slimming. Fliers are put on everything he can find, lined up along the street behind him as evidence of the progress he's made. At the end of a lot, he staples again.

At the corner of the road, an elderly man exits his house. The man's blue pants are pulled high around the belly. He waddles with purpose towards Jeremiah, brushing his hand across his neatly parted hair. A heavy breath is in his chest as he walks closer, perspiration dabs his face. The man raises his hand up, begging for a moment more of patience from Jeremiah who has stopped after a loud call of, "Excuse me there, sir."

"What?" Jeremiah's eyes are sharp.

Between shortened breaths, the old man explains, "I see you're putting up lawn sale signs of some sort."

"No. My son is missing."

"Oh. Well, let me take a look." A wrinkled pale hand extends.

Jeremiah provides a flier. The old man gives consideration to the picture, but shakes his head in conclusion. Jeremiah takes the flier back.

The old man says, "Well, now, I sure am sorry about that, I truly am. Breaks my heart. But putting up those fliers all over the neighborhood takes away from the image we're trying to portray here at Meadow's End. You see, I'm on the Housing Authority Commission," he states, "and we try to keep a clean neighborhood. It's our reputation. Fliers hurt that reputation."

"My son is missing." Jeremiah glances up the street, hand to his brow. "I'm putting up fliers to try and find him. I'm just hoping someone in this neighborhood might see him or have some idea of where he is or help in some way."

"I know, I know." The old man states, looking down at his mailbox and shaking his head at something displeasing. "But you have to understand that while I'm very sorry about your son, I truly am, we have a certain expectation to uphold. If I don't hold a standard, then no one will."

Jeremiah looks at the clock on his phone, then sifts through the backpack.

The old man responds to Jeremiah's lack of care, "I'm not going to ask you take them all down, but I will ask you not to put anymore up."

"I'm not taking any down. I will be putting more up."

The heat – along with the lack of respect demonstrated by Jeremiah – puts red on the man's face. "If you don't take them down, I will."

Jeremiah steps towards the man. The old man stiffens. Jeremiah says, "Don't you dare take them down."

"Are you threatening me?"

"My son is more important than –" Jeremiah looks over the visible parts of the neighborhood with disdain "– this."

"Your son is important. I'm not saying he isn't. But we have a standard."

Jeremiah moves past, even as the man tries to place a palm of consideration in his way. Trekking further on, Jeremiah ignores the feeble threat from the old man about making a phone call to officer so-and-so at the police department whom he personally knows. Jeremiah doesn't care. Call the police. If they're as much a help to the old man as they've been to him, then Jeremiah has nothing to worry about.

Jeremiah grunts at the blister on his foot as he continues jogging, stapler ready. It slides in his sweaty palm as he raises it for four clicks. He jogs again. His chest heaving. The exertion is melting him, the sun above. He pauses, hands on his knees, bent over with sweat dripping from his brow down to the dust and dirt and gravel. He catches his breath. He stands, knowing every second counts.

He glances at his phone again. "One hour," he reminds himself of the appointment he has with Detective Jamison.

Coming to the first light post on Hope Mill Road, he staples again, *click, click, click, click*. Up ahead, a couple of women approach. They walk with hop in their step, arms swinging at their sides, spandex shorts and sports bras. Jeremiah labors up to them with a flier extended. The paper drinks up the sweat of his fingertips. The taller of the two says immediately with a wave, "Oh, Sugar, we don't want nothing," as the two of them attempt to move past.

Jeremiah pauses, quickly figuring they've taken him for an old-fashioned salesman going door to door, selling vacuums or insurance. "No, no, my son is missing. I'm trying to find him."

His words crumbles out like an unknowing confession, and Jeremiah feels close to breaking down as tears rim his eyes with the declaration, the strange reminder from his own mouth of what life has become. He forces the tears away. No time for them.

"Oh, well then, let me see one of them," she reconsiders with a snap of her gum.

"He is a beautiful boy," the other one says as she looks the same flier over.

The taller one agrees, "Yes, he sure is handsome. Those eyes are some kind of stunning. What a smile," she exclaims, turning her face to her friend for agreement.

"He's missing," Jeremiah says again, trying to bring them to the reality that is his own, attempting to cut beneath their floating words. "Please, have you seen him?"

The shorter providers him a moment's pity. A moment's understanding. "No, I'm sorry." She assures, "I will definitely keep my eyes open. Give me a few of those fliers so that I can give them out to other people as well."

He does. "Thank you."

The taller one says, "I'll take some, too."

"Sure," he answers. He gives her just a couple. He can see her need to be like her friend, as if his missing son was nothing more than a colored ribbon and she's interested in showing her personal effort for the cause. "We will definitely be looking. We walk now three days a week and if we see him we'll be sure to call," she offers, as if Cole might be found on a stroll himself, burning calories.

Jeremiah offers his thanks. He's jogging again, knowing he can probably get about five more done before he needs to head back home.

15

A knock at the door. Jeremiah glances at the side window with momentary excitement at the possible answer of hope. He can't help but imagine a police officer with Cole at his side. He can almost picture Cole smiling as he holds the officer's big gentle hand, peeking up through the window to glance inside at his family.

Langdon is there, waiting.

Jeremiah announces to Bri, "It's Langdon. I'll let him in."

Bri leans in from the kitchen as she dries a cup. "Okay good. Ask him about the fliers I gave him and make sure you ask him if he needs more."

"Sure."

"Hey," Langdon greets as he pushes his way inside. Marching to the center of the living room, Langdon provides an immediate update, "I hit about five neighborhoods with all of the fliers I had. I think I had around two hundred. They're all up. I stopped by the stores and gas stations in the area too and talked to some people and gave them fliers as well. Also, I spent a couple of hours at the mall talking to people and handing out fliers there. That's where I ran out. I'll probably go back there later. The mall was packed."

Jeremiah asks, eager for a morsel, "Did anybody know anything?"

Langdon looks at his feet. "No."

"Anything at all?"

"No. Sorry."

"It's okay." Jeremiah hates that he had any hope at all.

Langdon asks, "What's next? Any updates from the police?"

Jeremiah says, "Let's go out back to talk."

"Sure."

Langdon goes out of the back door. Jeremiah stops in the open doorway as Bri calls from the kitchen, "Why are you going outside?"

"To talk."

"Why not stay in here?"

"We'll just be a minute."

He shuts the door. Bri shakes her head in hurt. Jeremiah has ignored her lately, treating Bri as though she were somehow an obstacle in his way, or maybe a painful reminder of what is. She goes back into the kitchen.

Stepping out onto the back deck, the planks of the porch are splintered and shredded, snagging at Jeremiah's shoes as he walks to the feeble railing. Before spring, Jeremiah had promised Bri that repairing the deck would be a priority. He had even bought wood in preparation, still piled near the fence. It seems strange to recall. Strange that it ever mattered.

Leaning against the crook of the railing, Langdon's bald head is burned red, forehead peeling in ashen flakes from the days spent outside in search for Cole. His face is beaded with sweat and his white shirt is nearly transparent with perspiration, drenched and sagging beneath the unending sun.

A hot breeze swings the screen door against the outside wall. It bangs again. Eyeing the nuisance, Jeremiah returns to the door and attempts to shut it, but it clanks, unclosed and swinging back to him. He shuts it harder, but it only clanks again. He examines the handle. It's broken – the tip of it somehow tilted to where it hits the doorframe instead of latching. He slams it again. And again.

"Don't think that will fix it," Langdon offers.

Jeremiah leaves the door against the outside wall where it continues to swing as he returns to the railing.

Langdon asks, "Any updates?"

"No." Jeremiah faces the open backyard. Gavin is playing near the swing-set Jeremiah and Langdon built years ago – just before Cole was

56

born. Jeremiah watches as Gavin digs holes with his Tonka truck. Gavin's knees are in the dirt. He rolls the vehicle up a bridge he's made with leftover planks given to him by Jeremiah. Straightening up from his play, Gavin calls with a wave, "Hi, Papa!"

"Hey, Gavin," Jeremiah greets.

"Did you find Cole?"

A strange pain. "No."

"Do you think he'll be back today?" The boy asks with his hand to his brow and his body layered in varying thickness of dirt.

"I don't know."

The boy calls, "Hey, Uncle Langdon."

"Hey, Gavin," Langdon greets with a smile.

"Your head is super duper red."

Langdon laughs. "I know. It doesn't feel too good either."

"Are you trying to help find Cole, too?"

"Yes."

"Okay, good."

"Papa, want to –?"

Jeremiah raises a hand to hush his son. "That's enough. Me and Uncle Langdon are going to talk." He turns his attention back to Langdon and says, "We just met with the detective about an hour ago."

"How'd it go?" Langdon bites his lip, already sensing the answer.

Jeremiah kicks at an upstretched splinter in the deck, ripping it from the sunbaked wood. "I don't know. She barely had any answers on what they're even doing to find him. So useless." He kicks again. "She says they've followed up on the few people they have listed on the sexual predator registry, or whatever it's called, but there were no leads. I think she only comes by because I bug her all the time for updates. I must call her at least ten times a day. It's funny. I called the police when it happened, and she came by and I couldn't help but think, 'Good, now Cole will be found.' But he's been gone for days." Dread sinks Jeremiah's knees as he realizes, "It's been two weeks."

Irritated with the detective himself, Langdon asks, "Did she say anything else? Any updates at all?"

"She told us to be patient." Jeremiah almost laughs. "She told us to keep doing what we're doing, putting up fliers and stuff like that. She says to be hopeful."

"I'm sorry."

"She said they're doing everything they can, but they're not, Langdon. There's no way." He watches Gavin place wooden planks around the bottom square of the swing set. The boy's jeans are too short, showing most of his high white socks as he leans the planks side-by-side in a makeshift wall with planks that are taller than Gavin, causing him to wobble and struggle for control at times as the wood threatens to topple him.

Langdon asks, "What makes you say that?"

"Say what?"

"That they're not doing everything they can."

Jeremiah states, "Because they're not."

"What do you want them to do?"

Jeremiah grits his teeth. "I want them to have every cop looking for Cole, and I don't want them to stop until they bring him back."

"I know. But we can't depend on them, and you know it.:

"I know."

"How are Gavin and Bri? Is Abigail even old enough to understand? Probably not, I guess."

"I don't think she does. Last night at dinner, Abigail kept pointing at Cole's seat when we sat down for dinner. She can't understand, but she knew he was missing. Bri is strong. She keeps everything going. She's there for Gavin and Abigail. She's doing everything she can to help out too. She has a Facebook page going. She makes phone calls." Jeremiah confesses, "But I avoid her a lot."

"Why?"

Jeremiah shows his shame. "Because she wants to cry with me."

"What's wrong with that?"

"Nothing."

"So why are you avoiding her?"

"I don't know." Jeremiah almost surrenders to the rising tears that flood him unexpectedly. "I don't know."

Langdon can see the pain. "How's Gavin?" He asks, hoping with each name to remind his friend of the people who love him.

"He's not doing good. He asks when Cole is coming back. He sits on the couch with his blanket a lot, watching the door. He wants me to spend time with him." Jeremiah considers the ineptness of everything he does, the excessive failings of who he seems to be.

"You need to spend time with him."

"I know."

"He needs you."

"Cole needs me."

"I know." Langdon urges, "Your family needs you too. They love you. You need to be here for them. You need to be out looking for Cole, but you need to be here too, Jeremiah."

Mosquitos have found Jeremiah, circling and buzzing by his ears. He slaps one on his arm. More seek his bare skin. The nuisance of their presence makes his response harsh as Jeremiah says, "You don't think I know that? You don't think I *want* that?"

Langdon remains composed. Gentle. "Your family loves you, Jeremiah but they need you as well."

"How do I do that?"

"I don't know."

"Then don't tell me what I need to do!"

"I love you, Jeremiah. I love your family. I know how you get, and I want to make sure all of you are okay, so that everything will be okay when Cole comes home."

Jeremiah apologizes, "I know. But I don't know what to do. I don't know what to do. I just want Cole home. I can't stop thinking about what happened. It's my fault, Langdon. If I could go back."

Langdon cautions, "You can't think like that."

"It's all I think about."

Langdon assures, "We'll find Cole." He then asks, "What's next? What can I do to help?"

Jeremiah coughs away a sob. "I've printed a lot of fliers. There's a stack upstairs. I'm going to local gas stations and stores and asking people if they've seen him. I've also been asking people I see and knocking on doors. Handing out fliers and asking for people to stay aware. Putting fliers on posts. If you could keep doing what you've been doing, that would be great." Jeremiah has filled his days with such, every minute he can, and yet saying it feels futile. He shakes off the feeling immediately, telling himself he's done much with much more to do, and the earth feels so big.

Langdon says, "Give me as many fliers as you can. I've got enough caffeine pills to keep me up for weeks. Finally, all those useless shifts in the Navy have paid off."

"What about your job?"

"What about it?" Langdon asks with a scowl.

"Do you have the vacation time?"

"Would you shut up? I quit my job. I can always get another one."

Gavin calls from the dirt, "Papa! Want to come see the castle I built for us?"

"Not right now," Jeremiah answers from the deck. "In a minute."

Gavin explains loudly, calling across the yard, "It's a castle I built for us to live in so that the bad guys can't get us. But we won't live in it until Cole comes back home."

"Okay, great."

"Do you like it?"

"I do." Jeremiah barely looks.

Gavin returns to his work after another dismissive wave from his father.

Langdon offers, "Go spend time with Gavin."

"I can't."

"Just a few minutes."

Jeremiah turns sharply on Langdon and says, "I can't! I've already wasted enough time."

"Is that what this was? Wasting time?"

"We've been talking for twenty minutes now, and yeah, in a way, we're wasting time."

"I'm sorry you think that." Langdon offers, "I'm praying. Every minute I'm out there, I'm praying."

Jeremiah turns his eyes down, as if turning away from something unseemly. Despite the countless blasphemies he'd love to utter, he maintains restraint, but he punches the deck railing, catching an unseen nail that gashes his fist and rips a flap of flesh away. Blood pours from the gory hole.

"You're bleeding pretty badly."

"I'm fine."

"You sure?"

"Yes."

"Of course you are. Is there anything else you need? Anything from me?"

"Not that I can think of."

"Okay. I'm going to go get those fliers." Langdon is at the door. "I can see what's happening to you, and I'm scared you'll kill yourself in your search to find Cole."

"I can't die yet, not until Cole is back."

Langdon states in all seriousness, "That's right."

Before Langdon goes inside, Jeremiah offers, "Thanks."

"For what?"

"Everything."

"Thank me when Cole is back. But don't thank me then either because that'd be stupid. Now shut up and go give Gavin a hug. I'll catch up with you later tonight to let you know how it went at the mall. If you want to talk at all, I'm here. I'm always here. Stay with us, Jeremiah. Don't drop away to that place you go to sometimes."

Jeremiah nods.

Langdon goes inside.

Jeremiah places both hands atop the railing, resting heavily with his head between his shoulders. Blood courses from his hand, dripping down to the splinters. He swipes the wound over his jeans in a red and black smear. It drips still. After enough time has passed for Langdon to have left, Jeremiah turns to go inside.

Gavin calls out, "Papa, come see my castle!"

Jeremiah wants to stay. He wants to be with Gavin, to play like they used to. But there's no time.

From his castle, Gavin watches Jeremiah shut the door. He's pretty sure Papa didn't hear him. Gavin returns to digging the moat around the castle – a moat where he can put alligators that will eat the bad guys who come after them. He'll show Papa the castle later because Papa will like the castle a lot. Gavin wonders if Papa will find Cole today so that they can eat dinner together and maybe play Legos before bed. He thinks Cole will like the castle, too. He scratches at a bug bite on his leg and says, "Stupid bug." Then he goes back to finishing the moat with his red plastic shovel, digging in the yellow afternoon sun.

16

The back doors of the dealership shut. Jeremiah drops against them like an escaped convict ducking from spotlights and searching boots. People inside the dealership cram every inch of the white tiled floor as they point fingers in excitement of things shiny and new. At the other end of the dealership, the double doors open again. Two more families enter. Then another couple. It's Saturday. Jeremiah is annoyed that he didn't think of such a simple fact. His anxiety races at the sight of so many faces. He considers leaving. He could have called Emad to explain things. But with the patience and sincerity Emad has always shown him, a face-to-face is not only courtesy, but necessary. He steps away from the doors.

With his chin low and shoulders up – as though shielding himself from rain – Jeremiah moves through the dealership. He remains discreet enough to remain unnoticed by the few familiar people he sees. People are focused on other things. Loud conversations. Sales pitches. Smiles and contractual handshakes.

At the center of the showroom floor, Jeremiah stands near the newest vehicle, scanning the price tag to provide himself an opportunity to glimpse where Komyar is, along with any other familiar face he'd prefer to avoid. Jeremiah is startled by a hand on his shoulder. Terrell is at his side. Terrell asks in a refined way, learning the trade, "You'd look fantastic in this vehicle, sir. Let's make it yours today."

Jeremiah turns, tossing his shoulder to shake away the unwanted touch, but before he can pretend too well that he's just a disagreeable customer, Terrell recognizes him. "Jeremiah, where've you been, man? You been sick or something?"

"Yeah." Jeremiah walks toward the back of the vehicle, his nerves commanding him.

"Oh, okay. Well, I hope you feel better soon," Terrell offers.

"Thanks."

With a clear path before him, Jeremiah walks to Emad's office. Through the open door, he drops into a seat across from the empty desk while putting his body away from the window as best he can, edging himself into the corner. Jeremiah waits, staying hidden. He hopes Emad comes in soon. Looking at the pictures of Emad and his family placed out across the desk, Jeremiah can't help but be happy for him. Emad, who escaped his country during the revolution in Iran, came from nothing and less than nothing. In America, Emad began by working at a gas station, quickly gaining position and responsibility while saving money until he eventually bought that same gas station. Then he began selling cars, every year bringing in more business. He purchased property nearby. Like a game of Monopoly, Emad bought more, identifying a deal in his favor, negotiating it into a better deal, and then ensuring growth through tireless oversight. A year ago, Emad bought this failing car dealership from a scoundrel who smiled at the over zealous, dark-skinned foreigner who was in way over his head. Looking over it all, Jeremiah realizes that today is the anniversary of that purchase, and Emad has turned that failure into a booming business that continues to grow each day.

Emad comes through the office door. His greeting is more professional than Jeremiah hoped, straight to business, "Jeremiah, you have not returned my calls. You've missed three weeks of work. Everyone tells me to fire you. I tell them 'no.' Tell me why I'm right." Emad sits at his desk, hands folded before him.

Before Jeremiah can answer, Emad leans forward to say, "Jeremiah, this is a very bad day for talking. You come in Monday morning. You shave. You clean yourself up. I'll give you work. You show up on time like you always do. We start over and pretend this never happened."

Jeremiah stops him. "Emad, I wanted to tell you in person, because I respect you and appreciate everything you've always done for me and my family."

"What is it? Are you quitting? You need to think before being hasty." Emad cautions.

"Cole, my son –"

"Cole! How is he? He is a very good boy, always with manners speaking with me. You need to bring him in some time. I'll take him driving in one of the newest BMWs I had brought in. If he's anything like his father, he'll love it."

Jeremiah's eyes falter and fall. "Emad, Cole is gone. He's been taken. We don't know where he is." Jeremiah's lip quivers uncontrollably, and he bites it, tightening his jaw.

In an instant, Emad's head drops. He stays bowed as if in deepest prayer, and when he looks up at Jeremiah again, tears are in his eyes. He apologizes, "Jeremiah, I am so sorry. Such a sweet boy, I'm so sorry." He apologizes for himself, "I'm sorry for being so quick with my words, you've always been an excellent employee, never any questions. I'm sorry for my accusation."

"No, no. Don't worry. It's my fault. You've been so busy, and I feel terrible about missing any work and causing you any frustration."

Emad raises a commanding hand. "Stop. No frustration." He then asks, "What can I do to help?"

"I just need some time off. And I want to make sure I have job when Cole comes back."

"No question. Always a job for you."

"I'm going to take every minute I can to try and find him."

"Yes, yes, of course." Emad pauses as he sits back, looking to the ceiling as if there might be an answer there to his contemplation. He says, "You take as much time off as you need. You will get paid for all of it. I will use my radio advertisement time to ask for assistance, it won't go far, just the local community, but maybe it can help. You will get me the fliers you are posting. I will send them to all of my stores. I will also place fliers here and have my staff provide them to customers and they can just say something simple like, 'please call if you have any information.' You can't be too descriptive with customers or you lose them. They have no attention. But a flier with his picture will be good, and your phone number so they can call." Emad then takes out a small book, scribbles in it with his pen and provides a check to Jeremiah. "Here's 3,000 dollars. If you just use it to pay bills, that's okay. However if it can help, make it help. If you need more, you don't hesitate to tell me." He finishes, "I'll do whatever I can."

Jeremiah stares at the check. "Thank you, Emad. I don't know what to say."

Shaking off the gratitude, Emad says, "It's nothing. Nothing. You find Cole." His eyes are gentle and intent, a man of will, believing always in simple things like determination and hard work as the answers to most of life's struggles. Standing from the chair, Emad reminds, "This is a very busy day and I must go." He looks at his watch, then at his phone.

"Of course." Jeremiah stands as well.

Emad says, "The thing is finding Cole. When you do, bring him here. We'll go for that ride." He smiles.

A soft grin comes to Jeremiah's face as he's given hope. His son will return. Emad, this man of means, has provided him newfound courage and optimism. The idea of this being over – of Cole coming here for a promised visit and a ride in a BMW – has him picturing his son watching the world pass by while zooming down the street with an exclamation of, "Wow! This is super duper duper duper fast!" – it strengthens Jeremiah.

It's just a matter of time.

17

They surround Jeremiah for guidance – a group created of a mixture of friends, co-workers, neighbors, and sympathizers – all of them on Jeremiah's front lawn with eyes intent upon him. People on the lawn in mass. There's a muggy haze over the land, thickening the air. Humidity resides between the trees and homes, making each face sweaty. Jeremiah can feel perspiration building beneath his own clothes, coursing down his body in steady streams. The sun is in Jeremiah's eyes, stinging him as it mixes with his sweat. He's nervous. He's never enjoyed talking in front of people, but who really does? But there's another nervousness, the same that has been in his ribcage day in and day out, fear that this too will prove useless.

The fliers he holds begin to wilt, and Jeremiah begins handing them out before they become too damaged. Jeremiah places stacks into each person's waiting hand, moving hastily through the crowd before too many questions are asked. He's not said a word.

Finished, Jeremiah returns to his original place just in front of the porch steps. Gavin stands behind in his father's shadow, as though he might be preparing for the same role when his father steps down from his position. As Jeremiah begins to speak, Gavin lays his head against his father's lower back, turning his face to the side. Jeremiah can feel his son's tired sadness. It makes him want to turn and carry his son to bed, sing to him like he used to.

Jeremiah explains loudly, "You've all been paired up and given stacks of fliers. They have the information listed of what you're supposed to do. I've kept it simple. In your teams, you're going to go to the designated neighborhood and go door to door to talk to people, tell them about Cole, and give them a flier. Please be sure to show them my contact information." He's cut off as Abigail fusses in her mother's arms from the porch behind. Bri drops down the steps with Abigail squirming in her arms, and she says softly in Jeremiah's ear, "I'm sorry. She's teething. I'm going to take her inside."

Bri goes to kiss Jeremiah, but he remains intent on the people in front of him. She kisses his cheek as if he were a stoic and unfeeling stone statue. She goes inside.

Jeremiah raises his voice again. "And for each team, I've provided directions to the neighborhoods you've been assigned to work through. Please keep track of which houses you visit. As you can see," he presents one in the air where it folds over, "each packet has a picture of the neighborhood printed out. Please highlight those houses you visit and talk to. The houses you don't get to or where no one is home, please leave *blank*," he calls out emphatically.

While talking and instructing, Jeremiah waves at the sun as if to swat it away. "Please prepare for a long day. This means a lot to us. Thank you. Are there any questions?"

A few arms are raised. Their simple inquiries are answered. Someone asks comically, "Are we allowed to stop for a snack if we get hungry?" There are a few subdued chuckles, but Jeremiah's dark gaze freezes them and a few people turn their faces down to the papers. Jeremiah notices the shuffling of unease, and he presses a smile onto his face, but it's distorted and plastic.

Pastor McDaniel steps through the crowd. He partially asks, partially declares, "Let us pray for God's blessing on this. Let us pray that Cole would come back to us, even this day."

Jeremiah moves to the side to offer his place, as though it were the designated spot for speaking and praying and other such formalities. Jeremiah draws Gavin up into his arms. His son lays his face against him. The young boy's meeker tone has Jeremiah feeling more inept, as though his flesh were thinning away, leaving him with less and less to offer those who love him. He rubs Gavin's back. Kisses his ear, then his neck.

Everyone bows their heads. Pastor keeps his invocation short, "Our God and Father in heaven, we give you thanks for the volunteers today as we labor in search of young Cole. We pray that wherever he is, he would be okay, and we pray that we might find him soon, even today, our great and mighty God, for you are able. In Christ's name we pray, Amen."

Heads are raised. Everyone pairs up accordingly. Emad comes up from the back of the group, and Jeremiah takes Emad's extended hand in both of his own after placing Gavin down to the ground. Jeremiah asks, "Who's running the dealership today?" as he peeks over Emad's shoulder to see familiar faces from the sales reps and even some of the lower level staff.

Emad states conclusively, "We shut down for the day. I'm paying everyone for their time. It was the most sure way of having everyone here. You know how people are." He glances over his own shoulder and nods his head after quick count. "Yes, everyone."

"Thank you." Jeremiah has little else to offer.

As he peers up to the taller faces of grown ups, Gavin asks, "Are you going to find Cole? He needs to see the castle I built him."

Emad's eyes glimmer as he kneels down to put his face level with Gavin's. He assures, "I'm going to try. I'm sure he would love to see the castle you built for him. I'm sure the castle is perfect."

Gavin explains, "Yeah, it's not as good anymore because rain kind of destroyed it some, but it's still pretty good."

"I'm sure it is."

"Maybe Cole can see it tonight."

"That is quite possible."

Gavin smiles as he's encouraged by the notion, and Emad gives him a hug. Emad stands again. His hand remains on Gavin's shoulder. He then turns and booms out, "Let's get going, people! Let's find Cole! Follow the directions that you have been given!" and he claps rapidly as the residual group shuffles away in pairs to their cars.

Jeremiah is strengthened. He can't help but think that maybe today is the day Cole returns. Maybe this night he'll be reading bedtime stories to him and holding Cole close, filling his son with promises and tears, apologies and smiles, helping him brush his teeth and singing songs to him like all the previous days of Cole's life. He's not sure why he would expect anything different. Why should he not have any hope? He thinks on Pastor McDaniel's prayer. Why would God *not* answer?

Watching the cars drive away to their assignments, Jeremiah pulls Gavin into a firm hug as he draws him up again, and he whispers in his ear, "Maybe Cole will be home tonight."

"I hope so, Papa. I hope so."

18

Abe and Diane Williams tilt their faces in the window that edges the doorframe as they peek inside, wondering if their knocks were heard and if anyone is home. Seeing Bri approach, they smile as though they were jolly carolers delighted to sing a song for whoever may open to them, a season of joy in their hearts to offer. Bri waves at them as she nears, then unlocks the door and pulls it wide. She greets Abe and Diane while standing to the side provide them an opportunity to come in, but they wait for Bri's verbal invitation.

Bri says, "Come in, please."

"Thank you."

They step inside. The early autumn air attempts to sneak in along with them, scooting past their ankles and feet. Cool air congregates at in the entrance.

Bri shuts the door.

Brisk pine aftershave wafts around in the entryway, carried about by the movement and motion of Abe as he removes his coat. He then draws his wife's coat from her shoulders. She thanks him. He nods in accord with his gentlemanly duty as such things were taught in his generation.

He then slides his shoes off, despite the carpet being marked in brown stains and grape juice blotches and other things.

Bri assures with a dismissive wave of her hand and a smirk that shows hints of her embarrassment, "Don't worry about that. You can keep your shoes on."

"Oh no, that's just fine," Abe rebuts as the second shoe comes off.

Diane laughs politely as she announces, "We were ringing the doorbell a few times until we realized it wasn't working."

Abe laughs along. "I kept pressing the button, but I wasn't sure if it was working. I even put my ear on the window and pressed it again. That's when we knew."

Bri explains meekly, "Yes, it's broken. Jeremiah hasn't had the time to get to it. Good thing I heard your knocks."

Diane looks to her husband. "I hope we didn't knock too loudly and wake the baby."

"I didn't mean to if I did," Abe apologizes. He brushes his hair, amending any possible disturbance from the gusts outside.

"No, no. Abigail is upstairs playing Legos with Gavin. Well, not playing really, just destroying whatever Gavin is making."

Diane offers, "I hope she's not putting them in her mouth."

Bri nods. "Sometimes she does. But Gavin is good about telling her to spit them out."

Diane questions, "She listens to Gavin?"

Her husband stops her. "Honey, Gavin is getting older now, and he's the big brother."

"You're right, dear."

With a thousand things on her mind as the day is ahead of her with tasks to do and a house to keep, Bri asks, "What brings you here?"

Diane stretches her pale arms forward to present a rectangular cooking dish overlaid with foil. She announces, "We brought you a quiche. We know you are in a lot of pain, so we thought we might relieve the burden just a bit."

Abe places a hand on his wife's shoulder.

"Thank you," Bri offers as she receives it, but her thanks is artificial as she considers her husband. Despite never being a picky eater, Jeremiah asserted early in their marriage that for a happy life together, she should never make quiche or "other weird stuff." Bri walks to the kitchen and slides the quiche into the refrigerator.

Lifting her head above the open refrigerator door, Bri asks, "Can I offer you anything? Juice, coffee, water? Did you want to stay a minute?"

"Actually, there was something we did want to talk with you about, if that's okay," Abe acknowledges, explaining further, "with the both of you."

"Oh, alright. Go ahead and sit down then. I'll go get Jeremiah."

"He's here? Oh, good," Abe responds, as though things were coming into place just right, a fortunate blessing.

Abe and Diane make themselves comfortable, sitting beside each other on the couch. Abe removes his glasses a moment, indentations left in the bridge of his nose, but before he can take his kerchief to wipe the lenses, Diane kindly removes them from his hand and cleans the lenses for him in tiny circles. Abe offers his wife thanks, then cuddles her close with an arm across her shoulders. She kisses him.

Upstairs, Bri peers into the darkened bedroom where the shades are drawn shut and the blinds closed. The ceiling fan and bathroom fan are on, filling the room with a steady methodical humming meant mean to provide Jeremiah as much quiet as possible so he can sleep undisturbed. Bri calls quietly, "Jeremiah, the Williams are here. Jeremiah." She stretches in further as she says again, "Jeremiah," this time a little louder. Her eyes adjust to the dim room and she sees he's not in bed, the sheets drawn down and empty. Muffled laughter from the hallway behind her has Bri turning around with an answer. She goes to Gavin and Cole's bedroom.

The sun pours through the clear and curtain drawn window, covering Jeremiah, Gavin and Abigail in bright warmth. The two children are too enthralled by their father to notice their mother as Jeremiah sits with them, building things. Bri smiles, hand on the door as she watches.

Gavin sits cross-legged, intently observing his father as Lego pieces come together piece by piece. Abigail stands behind Jeremiah, propping herself up against his back with her arms draped across his shoulder as she leans for support, her tiny legs just strong and steady enough to stand. Sitting there with creative intent, Jeremiah shivers visibly, his back and neck quivering in fatigue. Despite enjoying the sight her family together, Bri sees the tremors of her husband's body and can't help but say, "Jeremiah, you were supposed to be resting."

The three of them turn to look at her. Gavin is the one who explains, "Momma, Papa is building me a spaceship."

Jeremiah's voice is alive and gentle, a brief return to who he had once been. "Yeah, Momma, I'm building a spaceship."

Bri sees her husband's eyes, tired and sunken, like the eyes of a worn away strawman left for years in the sun and rain. But he looks happy, and she thinks maybe this is better than sleep. "Well, it is definitely a very good spaceship," she says.

Jeremiah goes to present it for Bri, but he pulls it away just in time as Abigail swipes out to snag a fistful of wing.

Unsuccessful, and maybe in toddler defiance, the small girl plucks up a Lego at her feet and shoves it into her mouth. Bri cautions, "Abigail, spit it out."

The tiny girl looks at Bri with her wide blue eyes as she challenges her mother's resolve with a toddler glare, and then turns to her father for his opinion. Jeremiah smiles, loving his daughter's sassy nature, loving the personality of his baby daughter as it shows itself, but he agrees with his wife in self-possessed joy, "Spit it out, baby girl."

After giving her father a moment's glare, a tiny scowl, Abigail spits the Lego to the floor in dribbles. Jeremiah kisses her, but the little girl shies away from the now bearded lips of her father who places the kiss near her ear, and she plops to the floor to avoid him altogether.

Gavin walks to his mother with the spaceship held out. "See, this is where the captain sits. And this is where the landing is. And these are the guns to shoot bad guys."

"What bad guys?" Bri asks.

Gavin looks down at the floor. "The bad guys, Momma."

Jeremiah interrupts, "Let's not talk about that."

Gavin returns to the edge of the dumped-out Lego mound and begins adding his own improvements to the spacecraft, small yellow and red translucent squares for added color. Longer pieces to add length. Bri announces to Jeremiah, "The Williams are here." She notices again his arm quivering as it props up the weight of his body.

"Why?" His tone returns immediately to its recent harshness.

Bri smiles as she attempts to keep the mood light and says, "They brought a quiche."

"They would." Jeremiah shakes his head. His smile returning.

"We should go downstairs, they're waiting."

Gavin explains, "Papa is going to build me a fire station."

"Papa can build it after the Williams leave," Bri counters.

Jeremiah encourages, "Tell the Williams' I'm not here."

"I already told them you were."

"Tell them I'm dead," Jeremiah says from the growing coldness within, instantly and forever regretting his words as Gavin sinks his head and drops the spaceship to the pile. The boy begins to cry.

"Jeremiah," Bri says in pain. "Why?"

Jeremiah scoops Gavin up immediately, standing to his feet. He rocks his son close, swinging gently side-to-side, offering remorse and contrition and promises. "I'm sorry Gavin. I shouldn't have said that." A tear drips down his face. "I'm sorry."

Gavin nods, swiping tears away with a fist.

Jeremiah sighs at his words. Sighs at himself. "I'm sorry."

Bri is hurt for her son. She wishes Jeremiah would never say such things. Doesn't know why he ever would. Jeremiah continues to sway back and forth with Abigail at his knees reaching up in jealousy, another Lego stuffed in her cheek. Jeremiah reaches down and plucks her up as well, but he soon feels tired, loose and woozy as his legs shake with a lightheadedness that overcomes him in a burst of stars. He sets his children to the floor to ensure he doesn't fall or drop them, falling to a knee with a hand on the bunkbed to gather and regain himself.

"I don't want to talk long," Jeremiah states as he stands again, shaking his head.

Gavin asks, "Will you come back and build more when you're done."

"I'd like to," Jeremiah offers before walking toward the hallway.

"Please?"

"I'll try. If there's time." But Jeremiah knows there won't be. Gavin knows too.

Bri waits behind a moment to offer a scolding finger to her daughter who stares back while sitting on the pile of Legos. "Abigail, spit that out." Abigail stares back. Both cheeks puffed out. Bri tells Gavin before she leaves, "Make sure she spits those out." The boy nods.

In the living room, Jeremiah sits in the chair with the tottering and broken-angled coffee table between he and the Williams. He offers a stifled greeting. Bri sits atop the cushioned armrest beside her husband. She smiles, hand on her husband's arm.

Jeremiah says, "I heard you brought quiche."

Abe nods and offers, "Yes, Diane has been thinking of you so much, and she wanted to bring you something." He pauses for an acknowledgement from Jeremiah – but receives none – and finishes with, "We hope you like it. It's one of my favorites."

"I'm sure it is."

Bri pinches Jeremiah's arm.

Jeremiah's irritation is rising. He has been interrupted. Taken from his children during a rare opportunity to be with them. And so much left to do. He's had such brief moments with his family and knows they need his presence – even if his seeming strength is nothing more than a mirage. And if not with his wife and children, he could be searching for Cole.

This is neither.

Diane states, "We want you to know that we love you two so much, and that our hearts are broken for you and what you're going through, and for Cole. We pray for his return every day during our family prayer." She turns to her husband who offers witness, verifying her assertion.

Abe declares, "We've spent many prayers, together and with our children, praying for God's will, and for Cole to be found by the police."

Jeremiah's throat tightens. "Why would the police find him?"

They don't have an answer. Just empty mouths that hesitate with confusion. Abe finally says, "I don't know how you mean. That's what they do."

"They do?" Jeremiah begs with surprise, but he restrains himself from further comment as he can sense his wife's apprehension, can hear her unspoken words of "be gentle."

Diane offers, "They do. There are many missing children out there that are found."

Jeremiah agrees, "They do find some."

Bri attempts to ease the tension as she breathes in the thickening air. "We're thankful for your prayers."

Their courage is built up by her thanks and the Williams are ready to reveal the reason for their visit. Abe begins, "After praying all summer for Cole's safety and his quick return, Diane and I were both convicted by something." He looks to his wife, and Diane nods at him to provide reassurance. "Well, we both came to the same conclusion, even without either of telling the other, we both came to the same conclusion and wanted to bring it to your attention. It's important and we know it may not be easy to consider, but you should consider it, especially because it may help bring Cole back. And that's all we want. Well, maybe there is some sin you have not repented of. Have you considered that maybe there is something from your past that is in need of repenting before Cole will be returned to you? To all of us." Abe rests his forearms on his thighs as he attempts to appear thoughtful and authoritative.

Jeremiah nods passively. His fingers dig into the flesh of the chair. Waves crash inside, stirred and riled.

Bri goes to say something, Jeremiah isn't sure what, but she escapes, a hand to her mouth as she flees upstairs in soft retreat. The bedroom door shuts. Jeremiah can hear her sobs from the bedroom above drifting down through the floor. He is hurt for her. Still in love with her. His eyes fix onto the Williams.

Diane promises, "We don't say this lightly, I hope you know, and we're sorry for any hurt our words may have caused. Bri is dear to us. I'm sorry for her tears."

Abe adds, "And we certainly wouldn't have said it if we didn't think it was important. But we both felt it was a word from God, a word that he wanted us to give to you. Like I said, we both came to the same conclusion."

Jeremiah nods. Dark hair and beard. Eyes severe.

Seeing the frozen nature of the man across from them, and hearing Bri's sobs in muted sadness above, Diane promises, "And we just want Cole back with you. That's all we want. We just want to make sure that there isn't anything stopping that from happening. Maybe some sin in your past. Something." She pleads, "It's been months."

"She's right," Abe looks at his wife, adoring her courage. "These are words given in love. Love is hard sometimes, we all know that."

"Yes, it sure is," Jeremiah agrees.

"And we thought we might pray with you, to help," Abe offers.

"I'd sure like that."

Abe leads them in prayer. Heads bowed. Abe declares the majesty of the Lord, His greatness and the glory of His throne. His ability to see. His ability to save. Jeremiah hears such words and cannot deny them – deep down he still hopes in them. Abe then begs the repentance of Jeremiah and Bri in the sin from which they must turn away, whatever it may be, so that God might finally bless this family. The prayer is finished. Abe wipes his eyes with the kerchief of his pocket. Diane dabs away her own.

Jeremiah's chin rises. His dark eyes peel thinly as he looks at Abe and Diane. As he speaks, his voice is cold and edged, like a jagged knife drawn from layers of ice. "I hope," they look at him with acceptance of his coming confession, knowing that all will be forgiven, "I hope your children are murdered. I hope they're abducted. I hope they scream and cry." He smirks. Unable to control himself or stop the pain. "You know, so that some sin of yours can be repented of."

Diane drops back with a hand to her chest in shock. Abe's cheeks flush an indignant red. Abe attempts to raise his voice, dwelling on the curses proclaimed upon his children, but the waves in Jeremiah spill over as they crash out with command, "Keep your mouth shut!"

Abe attempts to speak again.

But Jeremiah. Vehement. "You come here with your words. You think you come as messengers of God. My son, my baby boy, is gone!" He pounds a fist against his chest. "Cole is gone, taken by the hands of some man. And we're falling apart. All of us. Me. My wife! Gavin! Something we need to repent of? You come into my house! My house! My son is missing! You disgust me!"

Abe stands with a declaration, "You will ask forgiveness of me and my wife, and you will ask forgiveness for what you said!"

Jeremiah's fire freezes. He sits back. Cold and cruel. "You first."

Diane is at the elbow of her husband, pleading for him to calm down. She draws him near the door for exit.

Abe bursts out, "You will repent for those curses on my children! How dare you!"

Jeremiah stands. He takes a threatening step forward. "I won't. Now get out of my house before I show you the worst part of me."

"I am your elder of twenty years! You have assaulted me, my wife, and my children, and you will hear what I have to say!"

Jeremiah suddenly senses Gavin watching from the top step. He stops himself for the sake of his son and says with lighthearted amusement, "Leave my house. Take your quiche with you. No one even likes quiche."

Diane's coat is on, her husband's too. They exit with promises that Pastor McDaniel will hear of this.

After the door slams shut, Jeremiah turns to his son. "Sorry about that," Jeremiah offers to Gavin who walks down the steps towards his father.

"It's okay," Gavin says.

"I might have said some things I shouldn't have."

"Like what?"

"Never mind. It's better left alone."

"Okay." The boy looks up to the face of his father.

Jeremiah draws Gavin up into his arms. He carries him back upstairs to his bedroom where Abigail is pulling apart the spaceship with delight, flinging pieces to the side as though plucking feathers.

Gavin asks, "Do you want to play more Lego's with me?"

Jeremiah kneels down with a promise that hurts him. "I do. But I'm going to go see Mommy. Then I need to go. I'll try and play later. Okay?"

"Okay."

"I'm sorry, Gavin." Jeremiah almost falls apart right there, almost weeps. But he composes himself, gritting his teeth through a force of will.

"It's okay, Papa."

"Are you sure?" Jeremiah's voice trembles.

"Yeah, you can go."

"I love you."

Gavin smiles sadly. "I love you too, Papa."

"Watch your sister, okay? It's almost her nap time, and you won't have to watch her much longer."

"Okay."

Jeremiah goes to Bri. In the bedroom, the walls are dimmed and the ceiling fan still turn. Bri lays on her side in the bed, legs curled up as she stares at the pictures arranged atop the dusty vanity, the sheets over her ankles and thighs. Jeremiah shuts the door behind him. Bending to the mattress, he lays beside Bri and pulls her to him, unsure of how long it's been since he's done so. The smell of her hair and her skin bring memories of countless days together, as though there had never been a time that he did not know her to be his wife. Bri shifts her body closer to his. In the arms of her husband, Bri cries and cries.

19

Jeremiah sits on the couch scrolling through a webpage on his laptop for any updates from anyone that might have information. Any thread. Any needle. He spends most of his time scanning his way past condolences. He blinks often. Head nodding.

We're so sorry.
So hurt for you.
Don't give up.
Hang in there.
Keep hope.
Stay strong.
God will bring him back.
God is still in control.
We're praying
Cole will be found.

Jeremiah passes the words quickly by, as though they were shredded pieces of a life vest thrown to him while drowning. Just as useless. Almost mocking.

His phone rumbles in ricochet on the kitchen counter. Jeremiah orients himself towards the continued vibration. He almost stays, thinking that it will be the usual voice he doesn't want to hear, someone asking about this or that, someone trying to steal away his time with something useless, or asking questions meant to sound like sincere concern. Like they can relate to what he's going through, his family is going through. He stands and places the laptop onto the cushion behind him. His head lightens for a moment, causing him to grip the doorframe at the kitchen for balance. Stars burst in his vision. He picks up the phone.

"Hello?"

"Hello. This is Officer Blanchard over at the Raleigh Police Department. Is this Mr. Jeremiah Fray?"

The hopeful tone of the officer's voice causes Jeremiah to burst out, "Yes, yes it is," unable to control the exhilaration. He turns towards the windows, leaning over the counter. "Did you find my son? Did you find Cole?"

"Yes sir, we did."

Jeremiah can hear the warm smile on the other end of the phone and he smiles too, looking at the ceiling with a sense of new life, profound and free. Before permitting himself the joy that fills his chest with white warm light, Jeremiah asks, "Are you sure?"

"Yes, Mr. Fray. He's in the waiting room with another officer. He's eating a snack."

"He's eating a snack," Jeremiah repeats as if it were the most amazing thing he's ever heard. Composing himself, he announces, "We'll be at the department in about thirty minutes. It's called a department, right?"

"Yes, Mr. Fray." The officer seems to smile in knowing.

"Sure, sure. We'll be there soon. We're picking up Cole soon."

The phone is shut off. Jeremiah takes a moment as he tries to manage the flood of emotions, but it's like trying to embrace a waterfall. He wants to yell in triumph, yell and weep for joy. It's time – time to get his son – time to bring Cole back through the doors of their home and hold him and never let him go.

Jeremiah grabs the van keys and runs upstairs to gather the rest of his family. He calls out with everything in him, "Bri! Gavin! Abigail! They found Cole! They found him! Dear God, they found our son!"

20

They walk together. Hasty steps along the sidewalk. Gray tarnished clouds above. Abigail bobs up and down in Bri's arms. Gavin's hand swings with his father's as they scurry. They come to the concrete steps of the government building. The American and North Carolina flags flap in the wind. Jeremiah draws the heavy blue door open for his family as people come and go around them. They enter inside a chilled building of marble floor and high dull walls where stuffy air throbs in unmoving cold. A sign warning *Slippery When Wet* is outside the men's bathroom to the right with the door propped open. The janitor mops casually from side to side, a man passing time.

Taking their hurried path through the center aisle of chairs, Jeremiah and his family skitter to the information desk at the opposite end of the room where it stands isolated, like a single booth at the country fair Behind the desk is an officer on the phone. With his arm strung over the counter and his family just behind him, Jeremiah announces to her, "We're here to pick up our son."

The officer glances up from the computer while typing, a phone pinched between her shoulder and ear. "Just a moment please. I'll be right with you."

Gavin looks around at the expanse of walls and countless doors. He asks, "Papa, is Cole in this room?"

"I don't know." Jeremiah smiles at his boy, imaging the embrace his two sons will soon share.

"Where is he though?" Gavin asks, eyeing a solid gray door.

Jeremiah ignores the second question, and Bri bends down to answer, answering on behalf of her husband, "He's here in this building." Abigail smiles excitedly as she begins batting Gavin on the top of his head from over her mother's shoulder, as though playing a silly game.

Gavin asks, "Then where is he?" wincing mildly at his sister's whaps.

"He's here. They're just making sure he's okay."

"Why wouldn't he be okay?"

Jeremiah cuts them off, "He's coming back to be with us. He'll be okay. He's coming back home."

Gavin nods. Bri draws the boy to her hip.

The woman continues to talk on the phone, gathering information as she types, nails clicking rapidly atop the keys. Jeremiah asks again, this time with unmistakable contempt, "We're here for my son. Let's go."

Her eyes drag toward Jeremiah in a testy manner in order to provide Jeremiah a reminding recognition of who is in authority here. The officer states again, "Sir, I'll be with you in a minute."

"My son has been missing for months now. Months. They called us to say he's here, and we're here to get him. That's all. Please. We miss him. We just want him home."

The officer closes her eyes a moment, hiding any empathetic emotion she may have just felt, and says into the phone, "Sir, I'm going to put you on hold for just a moment. I'm sorry. Yes, sir. I'll be back with you in a minute. Sorry, sir." She hits a couple of buttons and announces to someone on another line, "Yes, there's a family here." She pauses, looking to Jeremiah for an answer, phone inches from her ear with her palm smothering the receiver.

"The Fray family. We're here for Cole."

She states into the phone, "The Fray family is here for their son, Cole." A moment. "Yes, okay, I'll send them over."

She points towards a room to the left and says, "103." She smiles. "I'm glad your son's been found."

Jeremiah offers her a nod of gratitude and a smile of his own. The family scuttles towards a waiting area where people pay fines and tickets.

There's a line stretching out around two separate corners. The line is long, filled with people irritated with the process. As they walk towards the metal door simply decorated with the number 103, Gavin asks, "Is Cole in there?"

"I don't know."

Jeremiah hopes this is not the beginning of endless doors and questions and waiting and more doors and waiting and questions. They huddle at the secure metal door until a buzz and a click signals that the door is now unlocked. Jeremiah holds it open as his family moves through.

They enter a more comfortable room painted a daisy yellow, with lamps and tables organized along the walls, above which hang portraits of police chiefs aligned together from years past. The floor is carpeted, a contrast to the slick marble in the vast room they just stepped out of. Magazines are on a table in the center of the room, allowing anyone who might be sitting to reach for a distraction to spend the minutes. Coffee brewed earlier in the day is on the counter nearby.

"Is Cole in here?" Gavin asks.

"I don't know."

Gavin lifts his blue blanket to his mouth.

A glass window slides open as an officer pulls it cleanly on its guide. Jeremiah walks to the short wall with his hand trailing a moment along Gavin's hair before leaving his son. A brawny officer smiles. Bray is the name on his golden tag. "You're here for your son. I'll take you to him." He disappears a moment.

Jeremiah calls his family to his side with an open arm and says while smiling, "Let's go."

A door opens and Officer Bray is there, his black boots shining. His workman hands usher them in with welcome as his smile remains constant just for them. Shutting the door, Officer Bray announces, "Follow me and I'll show you to your son." He quickly corrects himself as he states "and your brother," as he looks down at Gavin who then tucks his face into his father's side.

They walk past an organized collection of desks and chairs, a room busy of people moving about with phone calls, paper stacks, shuffling feet, and Styrofoam cups. Closed offices. Others with doors open. Fluorescent lights blare above. They pass the last door, coming around a corner at the opposite end of the room where there's a separate room with three snack machines, a long table for eating, and metal chairs. It's quieter here. The chaos of ringing phones, stepping feet, and varied conversations are behind them, like scurrying actors and stage hands making ready behind a stage. A single officer eats a sandwich, a paper bag tipped over in front of him. Past the table is a long window that spans from wall to wall where the tall buildings of the city can be seen. A lanky crane, clouds and sky. Sitting on one of the chairs at the end of the room is a child resting his head against a soda machine.

"Here we are," Officer Bray offers.

"Here we are?" Jeremiah looks around for another door.

Officer Bray presents with a hand, "Your son."

The boy at the end of the row looks up. He has blue eyes, his face is dirt covered. Red and blue Spider-Man shirt. The boy drops his chin into his palms as his elbows rest atop his thighs. He sighs. Bored.

Gavin asks, "Papa, where's Cole?"

"I don't know." Jeremiah's eyes flare as he turns on Officer Bray. "Where's my son? Where's our boy?"

Shaking his head at the naked incompetence of which he now finds himself guilty, as if the whole building has betrayed him just to make him look like a fool, Officer Bray answers, his tone stumbling about in confusion, "This is your son, isn't it?" He quickly recites the description, as if the fitting of terms and checklist might actually declare this to be their son and their mistake, not his own. "Caucasian male, 3 years old, dirty blond hair, blue eyes, super-hero shirt." He looks at the boy as he affirms such details.

Jeremiah states harshly, "That's not Cole!"

Bri drops her head onto Jeremiah's shoulder, wounded by wishes torn away.

"Where's Cole?" Gavin asks, his voice quivering with anxiety, "Who's that boy? Where's Cole?"

Shaking his head, the officer explains again, "I'm sorry. This boy fit the description. When we asked if his name was 'Cole' the boy nodded. I promise. We didn't have any other children missing with this description so we thought to call you. In no way did we think this wouldn't be your son." He then asks, "Are you sure?"

"Yes," Bri answers, trying to maintain politeness as her chest convulses with the single word.

The waves crash within Jeremiah, licking up his chest with growing violence, and he thinks he might be sick with their rising. His fists throb, curled up by his hips. He steps away, shaking his lowered and defeated head.

Gavin continues to look behind them as Jeremiah leads the family back the way they came, through clicking doors and out through the front entrance. The boy isn't sure why they're leaving without his brother, because they said Cole was there. They drop onto the concrete steps at the front of the building where the wind and darker air tosses the twilight and the metal clasp of the flag post clangs loudly. The family moves slowly, hunched with cold and despair.

Gavin asks, "Cole wasn't there? They didn't find him?"

"No," Jeremiah says.

Gavin asks again, "Then where is he?"

"I don't know."

Part Four

21

Jeremiah blinks. A day goes by. Maybe more.

22

He's sleeping. Maybe not. He's awake. He sits up in his car, having fallen asleep in the parking lot of a local store. Did he put fliers up yet? What store is this? What was he supposed to be doing here? He's putting up fliers. Why? Cole is gone. Keep going. Cole is gone. Keep going.

Jeremiah blinks. A day goes by. Maybe more.

23

Jeremiah places his feet to the gravel. The door of the SUV shuts with a click, a subdued sound that is somehow sophisticated, not the loud clank he's used to. Jeremiah doesn't recognize the vehicle. It's not his own, but with all the miles and hours traveled, he wouldn't be surprised if somebody let him borrow it. Probably somebody from church. Or Emad. He's thankful to have it.

Gavin is in the backseat unbuckling himself, his body visible in sketch through the dark tint of the window. Crawling out from the booster seat, Gavin climbs over the middle row and pushes the door wide with a small grunt. He drops out and shuts the door again with a shove.

Jeremiah isn't sure why he brought Gavin. The boy is bound to slow him. But as Gavin stands at his side, Jeremiah is glad for his son, and he thinks he should've included Gavin a long time ago, instead of keeping him at arms length. Jeremiah thinks *I'll bring him more often.*

"Is this where Cole is?" Gavin asks as he reaches for his father's hand.

"I hope so."

"Where should we go?" The boy asks.

"I'm not sure."

The question forces Jeremiah to plan and think, rather than moving around in his wandering desperation, like the destitute lost traveler he's been these past months. Gavin is right, and it convicts Jeremiah. Jeremiah needs to think about where they're going. Take advantage of every moment they have. Maybe he should have been planning more this whole time. But he stops thinking about that.

Jeremiah looks around at the tall pine trees surrounding them, lofty and thin, with sparse reaching limbs at the tip of their height where the needles remain above the ground to avoid the touch of men. Fallen, brittle needles crunch beneath Jeremiah and Gavin's steps as Jeremiah leads his son by the hand to a curb just a few steps away.

They pass beyond the forest's edge and walk into a clearing where only a few houses are in view, taking form with the nearness. The homes are aged, built of brick. The grass is a deep and healthy green, as though the soil is richer here. The neighborhood has the feel of generations, not like the common ones built so hastily where homes are jammed together with slices of lawn between where a reaching handshake can be accomplished from front door to front door by casual neighbors. No, these homes were put up with a sense of quality of life and discernment, separating themselves in seclusion from the rest of the world, made of better things, as the tall pines conceal them.

Looking at the brick front of one of the homes, Jeremiah pictures bedtime stories being read inside by a gentle grandfather as children gather around the fireplace with hot cocoa, parents looking on with tilted heads of admiration and love. Jeremiah shakes the image away. He's in too much pain to imagine happy families, as if any family enjoying time together is somehow a mockery of him and his.

Gavin asks, "Is that the home where Cole is?"

"Maybe."

"I hope so." Gavin smiles with expectation.

"Me too."

"Have you been here before?"

"No, I haven't."

"I like it here."

"It's nice, isn't it?"

"I like our house more though because it's where we live."

Jeremiah smiles. "Me too."

They walk up the driveway and onto a stone path where the dense aroma of freshly spread mulch pervades the air. A wall of well-trimmed bushes is on their right, green and lush. Up three brick steps, Jeremiah rings the doorbell. Despite being accustomed to the ritual of begging strangers for any information regarding his son, his stomach tightens, tightens like it does each time.

A woman answers, small and frail, her hair pulled back in a grayed out ponytail. Her eyes are round, abounding with wrinkles at their edges. She looks up at Jeremiah, awaiting whatever announcement he may have, and when he hesitates, she asks, "Can I help you?"

Jeremiah freezes, maybe caught off guard by her willingness to listen, and Gavin speaks up for his father, "Have you seen my brother? His name is Cole. He's kind of silly sometimes."

Her face brightens in an adoring smile, as though she's always found joy in the innocence of a child. She answers, "Yes, I have."

Jeremiah speaks with surprise, "You have?"

"He's out back playing with my son. They're throwing rocks into the water," she answers as though it were obvious, as if it had been agreed upon before.

"Can we bring him home with us?" Gavin asks.

Her voice is kind. "Of course. I know he's missed you. He asks about you often."

Refusing the urge to shove past and dash through her home to see his son, Jeremiah enters through the open door that she widens for their entrance. He picks Gavin up into his arms, relieved and excited, knowing that soon he will hold both sons, and his chest will be full with love again.

The woman shuts the door, then takes the lead in guiding them. They move past chairs atop a white throw rug, a stone brick fireplace, a wide mirror with golden trimmings rests atop from edge to edge, reflecting the entrance of their three figures. A long dining table is prepped for service, fine china and silver utensils. A golden chandelier above it. As they move deeper in and enter a kitchen, Jeremiah spies a large window at the back of the home. It's where they seem to be heading. He stares through the glass, greedy for a glimpse of his son.

"Our boys have played well together. My son will certainly miss having a friend," the woman states as they move down short steps into the back area of the home where the floor is gray tile. Shoes are by the wall, coats hanging down above them. At the door, the woman slips her feet into slippers and draws a sweater over her shoulders.

She opens the door. A strong wind greets them, pushing past as though seeking shelter from pursuing beast as it tosses their hair and ruffles their clothes. Gavin snuggles his face into his father's body to stave off the brisk gusts as it travels up their sleeves and reaches inside their collars. Pinching her sweater at her neck to keep it at her shoulders, the woman announces loudly to speak above the panicked gust, "They're right back here."

Jeremiah's eyes glisten with tears of expectation, like a just man released from prison after being declared innocent. He places a loving hand at the back of Gavin's head to press his clinging body tight. The woman, having remained just behind, closes the door, then walks ahead, leading them as she says, "Just past these trees."

The sound of crashing waves can be heard. The taste of salt sprinkles the air. As they step atop cobblestones, the sound of waves is louder, and moving through to a clearing, they find themselves at the edge of land. Jeremiah stands at a cliff, the height of which drops down to a gray ocean. The air is free and open before him, endless water spanning out to where it meets the horizon, the gray heavens high and long as eternity, devoid of sun or moon.

Jeremiah shuffles in steadied measure until coming to the height of the cliff where the wind cuts side to side and water sprays up from below. Toes at the edge, Jeremiah leans to peer down at the crags and crumbles of the rocky shore where water crashes violently. He sees Cole. His son, full and true. Cole is sitting on the smooth flat surface of a massive gray stone which acts as a dock for the boy. The waves slide atop the smooth gray rock in dribbles that extend, then recede again. Small puddles on the wide stone. Cole tosses pebbles into the water, just as they used to do at the pond near their home. He stands and throws again, his pebble going only a short ways before plunking down into the dark gray water. He throws another, then announces to the woman's son who stands along the sand nearby, "Papa would say, 'Great throw, Cole.'"

Jeremiah announces, "That's right!" from the cliff above, expecting Cole to turn and look up at his father and his brother with surprise and joy in those big blue eyes. But the woman's son encourages, "Throw again!" Cole picks up another pebble.

"Cole!" Jeremiah yells. "Cole!"

The ocean winds steal his words.

Gavin calls down, "Cole! We're here!"

Cole throws again. As he does, the water licks at his toes, then withdraws back below the rock's lip. Tempted by the taste, the water comes again, higher now, soaking Cole's shoes and laces in an ankle high wave.

"Cole! The tide is coming in! Cole!" Jeremiah yells as loud as he can, "Cole! Please!"

Cole takes advantage of the waves being away for the short moment, and spying another pebble, he picks it up and throws. The waves come for him, this time causing Cole to stumble back for balance. The water retreats.

Jeremiah screams fiercely, "Cole!"

Jeremiah sets Gavin to the ground and offers a hastened assurance of, "I'll be right back." Gavin nods with understanding, despite his fingers still reaching for his father's hand. By the time Jeremiah turns back around, Cole has disappeared from the slippery rock, as it too has disappeared, swallowed beneath the still rising gray. Frantically, Jeremiah cuts his eyes over the surface of the foamed and churning waves. He finds his son flailing much farther out. Cole struggles to stay above, splashing his hands. The water takes him, dousing his cries.

Jeremiah leaps from the cliff's edge. He drops through the open air, splashing below the water where the cold tightens his lungs and thickens his skin. Jeremiah pushes his way to the air above. Clothes drenched and heavy. He swipes hair from his eyes, clearing his vision. He kicks his way towards his son, crying out for Cole. He sees him, Cole being drawn further out by the thieving waves. Cole blinks and cries, splashing in the cold water. The small boy coughs in desperation, but he sees his father, and his eyes brighten with hope just before he sinks below.

Jeremiah drives through the waves, swimming through the black water. His arms stretch and pull. His legs kick. His lips are blue. Salt stings his eyes. Panting breaths of weary exertion bear upon him as Jeremiah swims to where Cole was, and he dives head first, pressing down beneath to colder water. He squints through the watery blackness for his son, seeking some sign of a hand, a foot. There's nothing. He returns to the surface again, spinning and searching. Gasping. Flipping around in desperate search.

Twisting towards the dry earth where the home of the woman remains, Jeremiah sees the distance traveled. The land is far. Gavin stands small along the sand where he's walked to. The young boy watches, unable to help. He can only wait. Gavin sees the struggle of his father. His father barely able to stay above the waves. The boy steps towards the sea, but Jeremiah screams out, "Stay, Gavin! Stay!"

Jeremiah's legs circle tiredly beneath him. He goes out further. He dives beneath the waves again, but there's still no sign, and he is witness to the dwindling efforts of his body, his limbs and lungs sucked at by exhaustion and the cold. He pushes further. He can't give up. He's searching. He cries out, pleading for his son to listen as the sky above watches, unresponsive and uncaring, "Cole! Please! Cole!" When Jeremiah drops below the waves, he finds it almost impossible to push his way again to the surface.

Water fills his mouth. He chokes and coughs on salt and sea. A few more yards out, and he knows the water has claimed him as well.

Maybe it's what he deserves.

A wave crashes onto Jeremiah, submerging him. He forces his chin up above the surface in one last act of will. He catches a blurred glimpse of Gavin standing alone on the shore, blanket to his mouth as his sadness and anxiety come together, soon alone, with father and brother now gone. Jeremiah calls out in desperation, begging forgiveness of his boy, "I'm so sorry, Gavin! I'm so sorry!"

A wave pushes him below one last time.

———————

Jeremiah wakes from the dream, laboring for breath. He stares around in a panic. Bri is asleep beside him. The room is dark. Curling onto his side, Jeremiah weeps and weeps.

24

"Why don't you sit? Nap? Something?" Bri offers as she snuggles Abigail close, rocking her.

"I am sitting," Jeremiah points out. He stares outside at the leaves and the trees blowing around in the brisk and colorless late autumn wind. He's avoided the calendar, but can easily see the approach of winter.

Bri shakes her head. Her tone gentle and imploring. "Rest, Jeremiah, please. I'm going to lay Abigail down for her afternoon nap. You should rest too."

He ignores her. Eyes outside.

Bri walks upstairs with Abigail. A few steps up, she hesitates to provide Jeremiah an opportunity to acknowledge his daughter and say, "goodnight." But he doesn't. Jeremiah doesn't even see his daughter as the tiny girl waves at him, clumsily shaking her arm up and down in excitement at her father who may as well not even be there.

Bri carries Abigail to her room. She draws the curtains over the windows. Draws up a blanket to wrap Abigail in. Sitting in the rocking chair with Abigail against her chest, Bri rocks back and forth in peaceful rhythm. Bri wants to cry. She wants to be angry. She wants to scream at Jeremiah and beg him to come back to them. Pull him back somehow. He's dwindling. So little of him left. She too wants Cole back, her son who looks so much like her. She wants to hear him call her "Momma," and to kiss him and coddle him and listen to all his grand stories about the day. She remembers the morning they brought Abigail home from the hospital. In this same room, staring at his newborn sister, a two year old Cole had asked with eyes of wonder, "Momma, is that *my* sister?" She had answered "yes," very aware of how sweet her son was. "What are you doing?" he had then asked. With tired sweetness, she answered, "I'm rocking your baby sister to sleep." He said, "Oh," maybe the answer not being much more than he expected, and she asked, "Do you want to kiss your sister before she goes to sleep?" He smiled. "Yes." And he kissed Abigail's forehead in untaught affection before bounding away.

Ushering Abigail to sleep in her silver and purple room, Bri doesn't understand how her son might not now just walk in and do the same. She keeps herself from falling away in tears, holding Abigail close as she sings soft lullabies. Bri looks down at the big blue eyes of her daughter and asks sadly, "Where's your big brother?"

Abigail blinks.

"I want him home, sweet girl." Bri's eyes drip tears. "I want my baby home."

After a prayer and a kiss, Abigail is in her crib face down, nuzzled into her plush bunny with her butt up in the air. The pink blanket is pulled up over her backside and Bri whispers, "Sleep well, Abigail." The bedroom door is shut.

Downstairs, Jeremiah remains on the couch. Staring like an invalid. Bri was hoping he would already be gone – though she hates to admit it. Really, she'd rather her husband be sleeping. Jeremiah is still human, with a nature of need, and sleep has been something he has not permitted his failing body to have for months now, as though punishing it, depriving it in self-loathing. His resolve is destroying him. Yet, it's what she hopes in. His will. She almost goes to sit beside him, to walk across the carpet floor and rest her head against the strong shoulder of her husband. His withered shoulder, she quickly notices. His frame has faded away. His shirts hang loosely, like hand-me-downs from a much older sibling. His cheekbones are pronounced. His growing beard does little to hide what's become of him. The sad sunken eyes. She sits on the chair across from him, putting herself between he and the window. She asks again, "Jeremiah, why don't you go lay down? Just for a little bit?"

"I'm getting ready to leave." He tries to sound more understanding as he explains, "There are a few stores I want to follow up at, and a neighborhood I want to check and see if the fliers are still posted."

"I know. You've done a lot."

His eyes creak towards her. There's hatred in them.

"Why?" She asks, lips trembling.

"*'Why'* what?" His voice is angry, damaged.

"Why do look at me like that?"

"I'm sorry." He looks out of the window again. "I don't want to. I'm exhausted. I'm just so tired sometimes."

"I know. That's why I'm telling you to go lay down."

"Cole is still out there," he states plainly. Through the window, he can imagine Cole outside, able to see him through the window as the boy sprays the water hose into the air after being told numerous times to turn it off. His son is not there. The window vacant of him.

Bri asks, "And what about us? What about spending time with Gavin and Abigail?'

He looks away. "I can do that when Cole is home."

"Just for a little bit. I know Gavin would like it. He's strong. He knows you're out there looking for Cole, but he asks when you'll be back to spend time with him."

The creases in Jeremiah's face soften. His lips tremble and his eyes take on pain and hurt. But the previous coldness returns and he explains, "There is this part of me that says to do that. It tells me to return to how things were, to pretend, even a little. It tells me to spend time with my family, to go to work, come home, eat dinner, and rely on the police or someone else to bring Cole home. Sometimes, I tell myself that I've done everything I can. Because there's that part of me that wants to be here. I want to hold my children. I want to hold you," he confesses. "But then I picture Cole alone somewhere. A shadow of a man over him. And Cole crying. I picture Cole in some corner of a basement, dirty and hungry, crying as some man takes advantage of him. Probably in some home I've passed numerous times."

Bri is aghast. Disgusted. "Why do you picture that?"

A harsh look of knowing tightens on Jeremiah's face, as if nothing else could possibly be true, and he states, "Because that's likely where he is – in some cruel man's home – and *that* is what keeps me going, Bri."

The image produced by Jeremiah turns her stomach. Jeremiah is amazed that Bri truly never considered this, or at least never allowed herself to.

Jeremiah asks, almost in resentment, "Why haven't you blamed me?"

Bri considers her words before speaking. It's true. In moments of weakness, she's wanted to do just that, to allow herself to blame him, to curse and hate Jeremiah for losing their son. She answers, "Because it wouldn't be fair. Because I could have done the same thing."

"But you didn't. I did."

"It wouldn't help anything."

"It's what I deserve."

"No, it's not."

"It's exactly what I deserve."

"Stop, Jeremiah. Don't do this."

"Cole is missing because of me. Whatever someone is doing to our son, whatever pain Cole is going through, is because of me." Jeremiah looks down, unable to look up any longer.

"Don't talk like that, please," Bri begs.

"Why not?"

"Because it doesn't help anything."

"It's not about helping."

"You shouldn't."

"Why not?"

"Because you shouldn't."

"Do you know what *father* means?" Jeremiah asks.

Bri responds, growing frustrated with a conversation she never intended to have, "What Jeremiah? What does *father* mean?"

"It means *safety*. It means *protector*."

"Jeremiah, it's not your fault, and talking like this is not going to bring Cole back."

Silence for a short while. Both of them hold back things they want to say. His mind, vague like muddled water, has Jeremiah forgetting what they were talking about, like a sheet were drawn up over his face and body, but he remembers, remembers Cole sitting in a corner crying. He says, taking up the conversation again, "I can see us going to parks together, eating pizza on Fridays, going to church, the four of us. But when I think of doing those things, and I think of our missing son, I take that part of me, that part of me that wants to forget and move on," he grows loud, louder than he wants, "I take that part of me, and I put my foot on the back of his neck, and I press his face into the mud and suffocate him there until he's dead. I kill that part of me, because I will not allow him to have one moment of my time!"

"Jeremiah, believe me, I want you to find our son." Bri appears prone, legs and arms tucked to her body.

"Do you?"

That one hurt, going too far, even Jeremiah knows, and she points a finger. "Don't you dare, Jeremiah! Don't say anything like that ever again!" Her voice rises too. "I love our son as much as you! But I have to be here for our children! I have to be here for you! Don't you dare accuse me of anything like that ever again!" She turns away.

Jeremiah offers in apology, "I won't. I promise. I'm sorry. I am."

She quickly forgives. "I know."

"I'm so sorry." Face in his hands.

"Please, Jeremiah, rest."

"Stop saying that!" He yells.

"We need you. I need you. Just a little while," she implores, knowing it's now or never.

Jeremiah looks at the stairs. "Cole could be up there playing with Gavin right now. Everything I'm doing is useless. I'm useless. I'm out there doing the only thing I know to do, the only thing I can, and it doesn't change a thing. I put these fliers everywhere. I talk to people. No one knows a thing. No one helps."

"Langdon is helping."

The remembrance shames him. "I know. He's out there right now."

Bri says, trying to sound hopeful, "Jeremiah, we're going to find Cole."

"Cole has been missing eight months now."

"It doesn't mean he won't be back."

"It might." He almost weeps.

Bri's voices breaks as she says, "He'll come back. He'll be with us again. He will." Her words taper off.

"Maybe," he says just to hurt her. To hurt himself.

She waves him off, shaking Jeremiah and his words away as she begins to cry. Her voice robbed, Bri flees upstairs, leaving him behind and alone.

Jeremiah stands from the couch. He kicks the heavy coffee table. It flips over to the carpet, sending magazines and a cup flying as his shin explodes in pain. The pain feels right and good, as though it's the only honest thing in the world, and he steps on top of the tumbled over-table and kicks at the legs and table until all of it splinters apart in loud *cracks* and *snaps*. Abigail can be heard crying upstairs, awakened by his violence.

Wheezing and gasping, Jeremiah stands atop the shredded table, a pathetic conquering of screws and splinters scattered out over the carpet. He contemplates destroying something else, feeling like a maniac, but his son is standing at the bottom of the stairs. Gavin asks, "Papa, why'd you break the table?" as though there may have been some fatherly explanation.

Fists at his sides, breathing heavily, Jeremiah admits, "I was angry."

"Oh," Gavin responds. He then asks, "Were you angry because you miss Cole?"

"Yes."

"I get angry too. I get angry and sad."

"Me too." Tears stream down Jeremiah's ruined face as he makes every effort to hide the anguish.

"Are you crying, Papa?"

Hands to his face. "Yes."

"It's okay." The boy begins to cry too.

"I don't want to cry."

"Why not?"

"I don't know." Every word is barely heard. "I don't know."

"Is Cole okay, you think?" Gavin asks.

Jeremiah confesses, "I don't know that either. I hope so."

"You should try and find him some more," Gavin says with eyes much like his father's. His hair darkening too as he ages.

Wiping his eyes and face with a palm, Jeremiah steps over the crackling mess as he walks near his son. He wraps his boy in his arms and kisses him. "I love you, Gavin. No matter what happens or how I am, I want you to know that I love you. I always will. And I'm sorry."

"Sorry for what?"

"Everything."

"It's okay." Gavin rubs his father's back.

Jeremiah kisses his son again. He then gathers up the larger chunks of wood before sweeping up the splinters.

Finished, Jeremiah offers, "I'll see you tonight."

"Bye, Papa."

"Bye."

"I love you, Papa."

"I love you too."

Walking to the window, Gavin watches his father get into his car. He waves to his unseeing Papa as he drives away. Gavin stays at the window, watching for a while as neighborhood children run around and play. They ride their bikes, screaming in excitement. He used to play with them too. But he doesn't feel like it anymore. He goes back upstairs to his room and shuts the door.

25

Jeremiah sits awake in the darkness, his sheets tossed about and hanging to the floor. The sweat that coats his body is noticeable. Cold. The sheets drenched in it. His skin emanates heat. A fever. Like a mother's caution, he tells himself he knew this would happen, that not caring for his body would result in sickness. He pushes the correction away. Like shoving a mouth from his ear.

Despite the depth of night, Jeremiah begins thinking through the places he'll go. There are a few gas stations he wants to revisit to make sure the fliers are still up. A neighborhood as well. He stares at the dark empty wall, his eyes dead. His mind blurred. A tremble runs up his body. Maybe he should just sleep. No.

A small voice is heard from the hallway. Jeremiah looks to the door.

"Papa." A whisper. Coarse and dry.

Jeremiah stands from the bed, but has to steady himself as the fever shakes him by the shoulders and knees. He treads awkwardly to the door, hand at his head, and opens it slowly to avoid the squeak of hinges.

The whimpers continue in quiet tones, a voice locked away. Jeremiah flicks the hallway lights on to offer his son immediate comfort, to let his son know that he's coming for him, but the switch doesn't respond. He flicks the switch two or three more times. Nothing. A dark hallway. In the blackness, Jeremiah goes to the open doorway of his son's bedroom. Inside the nightlight glows, a dim offering against the darkness.

In the corner of the room, Cole sits curled. The small boy leans against the wall, knees tucked to his chest, arms wrapped around his legs. A moonbeam traces him. The boy whispers for his father, calling out as he slides against the wall. "Papa."

Jeremiah remains blocked, an unseen barrier will not permit his entrance. Held there, he watches the pleas and yearnings of his small baby boy. Cole begins to cry, sliding down to the floor on his side, sucking on his thumb. He hadn't sucked on his thumb in years. "Papa."

Jeremiah assures, "Cole, I'm right here. Look at me. Cole, look at me." He crouches down, begging for his son's attention.

Cole pulls his body into a tight ball as he continues to cry.

Jeremiah beckons louder, caged in the open doorway, "Cole, I'm right here. It's okay, baby boy. I'm right here."

Before drifting away into black and bleak dreams, Cole says, "Papa, please."

Tears streaking down his face, Jeremiah confesses in shame to his fading son, "I'm trying, Cole. I am."

Jeremiah is stirred awake by a streaking sun that cuts along his eyes. He's on the hallway floor. He slept at the entrance of his sons' bedroom. His head is throbbing. Heat pulses within his clothes, the fever remaining. Jeremiah rises on wobbling knees, hand to the wall. He's thankful Gavin didn't see him like this. Looking so pathetic. So pitiful. Struggling towards the stairs, Jeremiah goes outside to a world that hides his son.

26

The smell of Wal-Mart sickens him, like swallowing down a cupful of bleach. He's avoided this one place, but with few options left, he has to face it. He stands beside an employee, waiting.

With a small key, the employee unlocks the glass and pulls it open. Jeremiah moves forward to staple a flier of Cole up with the other pictures of missing children. So many. He can't look directly at any of them. Not even the one he puts up of his own son. Some of the fliers hold current day photos generated by the best assumption of a computer and its aging program. He wonders if one day he'll place one of these up of Cole too. He stops thinking about that.

Customers pass behind him, going in and out with carts empty and carts full. Jeremiah is certain they won't look at these missing children either.

The employee steps forward and closes and locks the glass again with a copper key. "Is that it?"

"Yes."

A burst of sadness startles Jeremiah, and he turns. A little girl, about Gavin's age, holds a rainbow monkey draped in her arm. She stares up at the picture of Cole as she continues to cry.

"What's wrong? Are you okay?"

She only cries some more.

With a sense of immediate protection, Jeremiah asks, "Where are your mommy and daddy. Let me help you find them." But he's raised to his feet by a massively powerful hand that's wrapped itself around his neck. Jeremiah grimaces in pain.

A gruff voice asks with displeased challenge, "Can I help you with something, fella?"

Jeremiah turns with a cringe to glance over his shoulder at the man. Bald head. Tattoos. Red beard. Massive shoulders. Jeremiah states through a wince, "She was crying."

A woman of uncommon beauty and dark flawless skin steps past the girl and places a hand atop the man's shoulder. "Penelope was crying, dear. This man didn't do anything wrong. Let him go."

"You sure?" Words made of sandpaper. Coarse grit.

The woman smiles with gentle assurance. "Yes, baby. Let the poor man go, Frank. He's just looking for his son."

Jeremiah is released, no longer on his toes. He rubs his neck at the aching throb pinned between the sinews and tendons. "I'm sorry. I didn't mean to make her cry," he apologizes.

The woman answers, "It's okay, dear. It's not your fault. Penelope sees things sometimes. That's just her way."

The ox of a man swings the small girl into his arm as though she were as light as the rainbow monkey she holds. The man asks, "What is it, baby girl?"

"Monkey showed me."

"What'd she show you?"

Jeremiah draws closer.

The girl points at the picture. "That boy is sad." Then at Jeremiah. "He's sad too. I could hear inside him. It was the saddest song I've ever heard – sadder than yours, Momma."

Jeremiah begs, "Do you know where my son is? Can you tell me anything?"

The girl answers, "Monkey doesn't know anything more. She wishes she did. She wants to. I'm sorry."

Another step nearer. "Anything more? From your Monkey?" He feels like a lunatic asking, but with little left to him, he'll grasp at anything.

"No. I'm sorry."

"I'm sorry, dear," the woman offers to Jeremiah.

The ox man says to his wife and daughter, "Let's go."

With her head resting on her father's shoulder, the small girl watches Jeremiah as they go. She causes the rainbow monkey to wave sadly at him.

27

Black Friday. Aaron stands in the long line for the pre-dawn celebratory opening of Best Buy, the large sign glowing yellow in presentation before the black sky. Aaron came early – 4:00am to be exact – and his eyes are tired from the unaccustomed earliness of the day. But he's giddy – giddy as everyone else in line as they all hope for a good deal. The reason they came.

For Thanksgiving break, Aaron has enjoyed a few days off from his responsibilities as a senior in high school. It's been just what he's needed, an opportunity to be pampered at his grandparent's house. No homework. No tests to study for. No Rugby practice. Just healing and rest. Laughs with his brothers. Lots of food. Plenty of video games. However, Thanksgiving has also meant visits and phone calls from extended family, and extended family has meant questions about Aaron's future and what he plans on doing with it. That's what family is for – to make you anxious when you don't need to be. But he's remained patient, providing uncles and aunts the individualized courtesy they deserve, despite answering the same questions over and over. He's on course to graduate towards the top of his class and currently waiting for his approval from the Naval Academy as a Freshman Midshipman next year. His parents would love that. They'd be proud. Family has offered him assurances that he'll be accepted, based on all of his accomplishments, his intelligence, his resilience. He's not so certain though. He's not even certain he wants to go. His brothers don't ask the same questions, and when they ask, they don't ask the same anxious way the other family members do. He knows it's because no matter what he decides to do, or if the Naval Academy accepts him or not, they'll still be brothers. That's all that matters. Aaron finds a lot of comfort in this.

A flurry of goose bumps runs up Aaron's skin, causing his arm hair to stand on end. A little dance moves his toes as the cold is at him eagerly. He can feel the chill on his cheeks and ears. It's his own fault for wearing a short-sleeved shirt. Everyone around him is bundled up, well prepared for the elements. Aaron smirks at that, thinking maybe it's a sign he won't be accepted to the Naval Academy after all, as his inexperience of life shows that he still needs his Mommy to remind him to wear a coat, to bundle him up for the elements. A gust passes over him, shaking him again. He laughs at it, laughs loud and hearty, as though mocking mild torturers.

His brother, Tim, comes from the parking lot. Tim shuffles along in boots and jeans one size too big, smiling tiredly.

"Hey!" Aaron says in surprise.

"Hey," Tim answers back.

"What are you doing here?"

"Keeping you company." Tim hands over a Starbucks cup and offers, "Here."

The cup warms Aaron's fingertips. He takes a sip. "Delicious!" He smiles. "Thanks, Brosef."

"Welcome." Tim sips his own.

Aaron says, "I bet Pops sent you here to make sure I don't get in trouble. Can't go and ruin Mom and Dad's big plans for me." Aaron nudges Tim's arm with an elbow and winks.

Tim's eyebrows are raised. "You think Pops would send me to do that?"

"I guess you're right. You'd be the last one he'd send."

Tim chuckles. "If he wanted it done right, he wouldn't send any of us."

Aaron bursts out in laughter. He then rubs his arms for warmth.

Tim asks, "Why didn't you wear a coat?"

"I forgot," Aaron admits.

"Still need Mom to remind you?" Tim smirks.

"Well, Mr. Felon, with all those prison tats you have, you must be tough enough to let me use your coat."

"I don't think so."

"C'mon tough ex-con, hand it over."

"Not a chance. Cold is cold."

"You sure, prison guy?" Aaron teases one last time.

"Keep asking, and I might shiv you."

"Whoa!" Aaron throws up a cautious hand of surrender.

The two of them shimmy closer to the entrance as the line draws up. The doors still haven't opened. Everyone is buckling together for warmth.

"I'm glad you came," Aaron says.

"Because of the Starbucks."

"Yep. Only because of the Starbucks."

"Thought so."

"And that's the only reason."

"I know."

"Nah, Tim. I love hanging out with you."

Tim smiles. "Me too."

"I was just kidding."

"Me too."

More cars park. Headlights brighten the waiting people in stark blinding light. Eyes close. The line continues to lengthen, bending at the corner of the store. After another sip, Aaron reminisces, "That first year you were in prison, it was hard. Holidays weren't the same without you." He states in realization, "Nothing was the same."

"I know."

"Thanksgiving was depressing. We pretended to be happy together, but you weren't there and then of course, Jaden started trying to make us all feel guilty for wanting to even act happy. So we didn't."

"Really?"

"Yeah. Anyway, we didn't do too much. Mom made food. Pops had things he wanted to complain about."

"Sounds like every other Thanksgiving."

Aaron laughs. "Yep. I wanted to get out of the house. So, I asked Jaden to come with me to Best Buy for Black Friday."

Tim interrupts, "You do this every year?" He looks disappointed.

"That was my first time, and yeah, now I go every year. It's worth it. Hater. Last year I got a laptop for about $150."

"That's pretty good."

"See?"

"Sure." Tim asks, "So, what happened?"

"Jaden told me he didn't want to go, just wanted to hang out at home with family. I told Jaden it would be fun and that he should forget about how much he hates crowds and all that so we could just hang out as brothers. He thought about it. Then he said he'd bet me."

Tim asks, "What was the bet?"

"Jaden said if I could name a movie a song was from, then he would give in and go. I told him, 'okay,' and got ready. Jaden played the song, and I was like, *'Silence of the Lambs.'* It must have taken me all of four seconds. I had just watched the movie the previous night, but he didn't know that." Aaron laughs. "Jaden just froze."

Tim smiles. "That's great. So, did Jaden go?"

"What do you think?"

Tim laughs.

Another sip. "This is delicious! What is it, anyway?"

"Pumpkin spice white chocolate mocha with an extra shot of espresso."

"*Piyah!*" Aaron calls out, pointing a finger of victory into the air. His body then shivers visibly as the chill air possesses him again.

"You okay?" Tim laughs.

"Yeah." Aaron laughs along.

On his tiptoes, Aaron glances over bodies and around shoulders for any sign of the front doors being opened anytime soon. He spies a homeless man up ahead working his way past the crowd. The man's greasy hair is disheveled in clumpy patches, his face covered with a scraggly beard, untrimmed and unkempt. Back bent. Boots loose. The people in line are unresponsive to the man as they turn avoidant and shopping-focused faces away from the shambling attempts at earning a sympathetic ear. The man seems adamant though, like someone intent on a message. Like Cassandra of Troy.

Aaron turns out his pockets for change. He then elbows Tim, telling him to do the same. After pulling together their money, Aaron asks, "How much do you have?"

"About four bucks."

"I have seven or so."

"That's decent. We giving it all to him?"

"Of course."

The homeless man steps near, wearing a coat too large, his wrists and neck thinned away and undernourished. His eyes shallow and desperate. Aaron attempts to discreetly push his fist of change and bills forward while looking for a bucket or hat to drop the money into, but a piece of paper is shoved toward him with words of, "My son is missing. Please call the number on the flier if you know anything or see him, please." The man then moves past with the same words and the same plea.

Cramming the money back into his jeans, Aaron takes a moment to look the flier over. On the paper is a young boy with blue eyes shining. The boy hugs the leg of a man – probably his father. The hand of the adult is on the boy's head, caught ruffling the boy's dirty blond hair. The boy is smiling. A moment of happiness.

"Should we still give him the money?" Tim asks.

Aaron answers, "I don't think he'd care."

Tim offers with realization, looking over the flier now, "You know who that was, right?"

"Who?"

"It's the guy Langdon has been helping."

"Are you sure?"

"Positive."

"What's his name?"

"I don't remember."

A commotion turns Aaron and Tim back around. A burly man has his finger in the face of the homeless man. Inches from him, he talks angrily. Aaron can't make out everything being said, but something comes out of the burly man, something about how this isn't the place for such things. He continues his acts of intimidation, growing louder. Those in line appear uncomfortable, some glancing around, while others keep their eyes forward, none of them wanting a disturbance during the holiday.

"Hey!" Aaron calls out while leaving his place in line. "Leave him alone. He's only trying to find his son."

"You believe that garbage?" The burly man asks as he stands upright, shoulders squared to Aaron's approach. "Don't believe this homeless guy! It's just a ploy to get people to feel bad so that he can come back and ask for money in a few minutes. I've seen it on the news."

Aaron offers, "His son is really missing. Our brother has been helping."

"Then your brother's an idiot."

Aaron continues closer and the man points in threat as he says gruffly, "Get back in line before I teach you a lesson. Punk."

Aaron takes another bold step forward, Tim just behind him.

"Back off," the burly man threatens more timidly.

The homeless man scurries between the three of them. He looks at Aaron as he assures, "There's no need for fighting over me. It's okay," and before he forgets, the homeless man offers, "Thank you, though."

"Get out of here!" The burly man commands before giving the homeless man a hefty shove that launches him forward. The homeless man stumbles awkwardly in rounded steps before falling on his elbows and knees to the asphalt in a pain-filled moan. The burly man declares, justifying himself, "Go back to whatever bridge you came out from and let us be!"

Aaron's fists are balled, his right shoulder cocked back, ready to swing and crack the square jaw in front of him. The homeless man calls from behind, fliers pinned to his chest as he stands, "No, no, no! It's okay!"

A security guard approaches, his girth bobbing with his hasty advance to the scene. Huffing, fists at his hips, he asks, "What's the problem here?"

"Nothing," Aaron answers.

Pointing with accusation, the burly man explains, "This homeless guy is running around with these papers trying to get money from everyone. I didn't come here for this, you know! I'm a paying customer, and I didn't wake up at the butt-crack of dawn to be assaulted by some homeless guy who just wants a drink or a fix or whatever the heck it is he needs!"

The security guard assures, "I understand sir. I can guarantee you that if I had known he was around, I would have asked him to leave." Turning to the homeless man, the security guard points to the world, "Sir, you need to leave."

Aaron raises his voice. "Hey! That fat ass shoved this guy! He should be arrested for assault." Tim nods agreement, his eyes having not left the burly man.

With a face of boredom, the security guard asks in a tone that matches his expression, "Sir, do you want to press charges?"

The homeless man answers, "No, that would take too much time."

"Then you should leave," the security guard says.

"Yeah, leave," the burly man agrees.

"I still have some more fliers to give out." The homeless man reviews his stack. "Probably about fifty to seventy-five more. And I haven't even talked to half of the people here."

"Sir, you're going to have to vacate the premises."

"It won't take long. Somebody might know something. Please. My son is missing."

"I'm sorry sir, but we do not permit the homeless to collect here."

The man states with a broken smirk of confusion, "I'm not homeless."

Aaron goes to speak again, but the security guard assures with a palm up for guarantee, "There is a scam among the homeless right now. It's very popular."

"I told you," the burly man states, arms crossed over his chest.

The security guard continues to explain, "They pretend they've lost a family member, or at times a pet, and they try to garner the sympathy of those around them. The first time through, they don't ask for anything, but then they go through the line or crowd again and ask for donations to help. It's very popular."

"Very popular."

"That's not what he's doing," Aaron replies. "Our brother knows him. This isn't a scam!"

"Langdon?" The homeless man asks, recognizing the discreet resemblance. His eyes tear up with the name. His chin trembles. He then turns to the security guard and the burly man and says, "I'm sorry for any trouble." Before walking away, he begs one last time, "But if you see my son or have any idea –."

"Damn it!" The big man booms out. "Just leave! My God! You just don't know when to give up!"

The homeless man walks off to the car filled lot. Tim stands near the burly man saying things that should be said as the security guard continues his attempts at maintaining civility. Aaron jogs off, catching up to the homeless man and meeting him at an old green car. Paint is peeling from the hood and the tires are dangerously bald. The back seat is covered with scattered fliers. The front seat too. The man turns to Aaron before getting in and asks, "Do you know anything about my boy? Probably not, or you would have told Langdon."

"No. I'm sorry."

The man nods.

"Hey," Aaron calls before the man ducks his head into his car. "I'm here for a couple more days. We're in town visiting family. Give me as many fliers as you want and I'll hand them out after that security guard goes back inside. Maybe they'll think I'm homeless too." He laughs, then stops.

The man digs into a bag and pulls out a thick stack of fliers. With thinned fingers and swollen knuckles, blood on his gravel-dusted palms from falling, he hands them over and offers, "Thank you."

Aaron assures, "Of course. And I'll call Langdon and see what I can do to help while I'm still here. Tim, too."

"Thank you."

After looking down at the stack briefly, Aaron offers, "I hope you find your son. Christmas is coming up, and I'm sure it'd be great to have him back in time."

The man seems to crumble apart on the inside at the words of attempted encouragement. Turning his grief to the pavement, the homeless man can barely say, "I know."

Aaron says, "I'm sorry," without explanation.

"It's okay."

The car drives away. Aaron returns to the store. He's not sure if he should start handing out fliers at the place where he was standing originally, or at the back. Walking across the parking lot, fliers are everywhere, dropped by those in line. Some are pinned beneath sneakers or boots. Others scattered between cars. Disgusted, Aaron grabs Tim, who is still talking in threat to the burly man, and they leave in their separate cars after Aaron hands his brother half of the fliers.

Aaron drives to his grandparent's home with resolve to give the fliers to everyone he knows, acquaintances, friends of friends, everyone in between. He'll do whatever he can to help, hoping his declaration is true, that by Christmas, the young boy will return and the family will be together again.

Part Five

28

With a frail sense of accomplishment, Jeremiah drives back to his house. He passes by fliers he has placed intermittently along posts and signs over the past year or so. The late February sun warms him through the windshield. The heats makes Jeremiah drowsy. His neck relaxes. His chin lowers. His head nods. He blinks. Blinks again. An abundant haze drifts over his mind and soon passes over his eyes, tossing him in and out of daydreams even as he turns down another road.

As if in a dream-like fog, Jeremiah can see the face of his son on every post he passes. Every street sign. The face of his son on every tree. His imagination creates more and more, multiplying them into a myriad of white fliers, the face of his son – Cole smiling from a time when smiles were true – covering the earth. That feeling of accomplishment he had a moment ago, that feeling of something done, flitters away, as Jeremiah is given the eyes of another person, of someone timeless, as he looks at these fliers placed by a man who lost his son. As Jeremiah looks through these new eyes, the eyes of a stranger, he begins to laugh. He sees the fliers for what they are. Nothing but paper. Paper ignored and disregarded. Paper passed by. Jeremiah laughs like a man mocked in ridicule to the point where he laughs too, and he shakes his head as he laughs harder and harder while driving along the windy country road.

Tears blind Jeremiah's vision as sobbing takes over. He skids off to the side of the road. Slams the car in park. Blinker blinking in his ears. Jeremiah lays his forehead on the steering wheel as he grips and shakes it in grieving fury. He weeps there as he imagines a thousand pieces of paper flying away into the wind, his son, gone and forgotten with them.

"Cole. Cole."

29

Drifting down the steps of her sleeping home, Bri walks softly between the dark walls as she goes to get a glass of water. The last step has her foot fumbling for the carpet as her fingers grope blindly through the open air of the living room until finding the light switch on the wall. Clicking it on, she's startled, hand to her chest. Jeremiah is just a few feet from her.

"You scared me!" She whispers.

"Sorry."

"What are you doing?"

Pictures are stacked in Jeremiah's left arm. The pile grows as he continues along the wall. He says nothing.

Looking around, Bri sees that Jeremiah is finishing up, as the rest of the room is devoid of family photos. Empty nail heads are sticking out from blue-gray walls. In her grogginess, Bri asks, "Why are you taking all of our pictures down?"

"I don't want to look at them anymore."

"They're pictures of us," she states.

"I know."

He removes the last one. Walking to the back corner of the room, Jeremiah places the stack uncaringly into a pile that leans and topples to the floor. Jeremiah walks to the kitchen and Bri follows him, coming awake as she does.

She warns at his back, "You are not throwing our pictures away."

"I won't throw them away. Not yet." He drinks some water, just for something to do.

She takes bait. "Not yet?"

Placing the cup in the sink, he stares out through the black windows and the nighttime there. "If we never get Cole back, I don't want to see a picture of us all together ever again."

Bri puts herself between Jeremiah and the outside, ensuring his attention and hoping he'll look at her, instead of through her. Jeremiah stares at the floor while placing his back against the counter, hands in his pockets.

"Why can't you look at me?"

He looks at her. Bloodshot eyes. Permanently stained. "I don't mean to not look at you."

"Then why don't you? Why do you avoid me?"

"I don't know."

"Did I do something?"

"No."

"Then why?"

"I don't know. I don't know." He grits his teeth at himself.

"I love you, Jeremiah," she reminds.

"I don't know why."

Her head sinks. "Don't, Jeremiah. I love you."

"I know." He admits, "I love you, too."

She almost goes to him, but she can see the dark nature of where he is, the seething heat emanating from him, the self-loathing. The pain. In an attempt to lighten the mood, she asks, "Can I put the pictures back up?"

"Please don't," he begs.

"Why not? I'd like to have them up. I love the pictures of our family."

"I can't take it."

"It's us, Jeremiah. We're still a family."

Jeremiah looks away and wipes his eyes. He confesses, "All I ever hear is Cole crying. He's always crying."

"What do you mean?"

"When I sleep, I dream of Cole in his bedroom, stuck there and crying. He's crying and cold and I can't get to him. When I'm awake, I can still hear him crying. Then he's in my dreams again. Crying. I can't ever get to him. I can't reach him."

"Jeremiah," she tries.

"I don't know what to do. The police are useless. I'm useless." He shakes his head slowly, admitting the conclusion he's avoided for days and weeks and maybe months, "We're never going to find Cole."

"We're never going to find Cole?" Gavin asks. He's standing in the doorway of the kitchen. He begins crying there.

Bri scoops up her son to comfort him, to guard him from the words of his own father. Gavin rests his head against her shoulder and says while crying, "I want Cole to come back home. I want him back. I want him back."

"Me too," Bri offers as she sways him back and forth. "We'll find him. I promise."

And when she says it, Jeremiah knows it's not true, and he's never felt so different from her in all their years together. He watches his wife with their son. He sees his son and the pain he has. He sees his son and the pain he has. "I'm sorry," he whispers. Jeremiah walks to Bri and slides his arm beneath Gavin, drawing him from his wife with a gentle word, "Let me hold him."

Bri releases Gavin and crosses her arms over her chest to cover herself from the emptiness there.

"I'm sorry," Jeremiah says to her. "I am."

She nods, then looks away.

Jeremiah asks of his son, "Do you want me to take you upstairs?"

The boy nods.

Bri stands in the kitchen, alone, as Jeremiah leaves with their son.

In Gavin's bedroom, Jeremiah lays Gavin on the top bunk. Gavin asks, "Papa, do you still love me?"

Jeremiah lets out a slow breath of pain. "Yes. With all my heart."

"Will you lay down with me?"

"Of course."

Jeremiah walks to the end of the bunk bed and climbs up. Lying beside his son, Jeremiah props himself up on an elbow as he runs his fingers through Gavin's hair, caressing his neck and starting again. Soon after, Jeremiah is lying down as well, arm around Gavin as they both fall asleep.

Coming in, Bri saves her whispers as she sees her son and her husband. She walks to the bunk and runs her fingers through Jeremiah's dark hair. It's lengthened significantly. Greasy. Snagged and knotted. His closed eyes are dark and hollow and sad. Just above the silence, Bri begs things of her husband's sleeping frame, begs him to remember, begs him to stay, hoping her words will reach him in his dreams. Maybe he'll see her there. Remember her.

The softness of the nightlight and the smells of the room make Bri hopeful that it can still be like it used to. She has to be strong for all of them. For Gavin. For Abigail. For Jeremiah. There's no reason to give up. Cole is out there. Cole will come home. Soon. Soon. He'll sleep again in his own bed, sprawled out like a cat in the sun like he always used to, his belly in the air and arms out. It's just a matter of time. Any day now. Soon.

Bending to the lower bunk, Bri tugs the blanket and sheet down, made neatly months ago in preparation for Cole's return. She crawls in. The bottom sheet is cold. The pillow cold. Cole's short blanket barely covers Bri as she curls up tightly beneath it. The smell of her son is on the pillow, the smell of the day, of dirt and laughs and popsicles. She begins to cry. She misses her son. Wants to hold him. Hold him forever. Bri stares at the twinkling nightlight in a tear streaked trance until she too drifts away to dreamless sleep.

30

"Sir, that's not the place for things like that," the store manager, Jim, explains as he walks, his steps tired. A long day of work has made his body heavy. All he wants to do is go home, watch ESPN, and have a beer. Maybe two. He's earned it. Especially after today where every little thing seems to have gone wrong. The shipment of pizza ingredients didn't come in on time. The credit card swipe stopped working on pumps three and four. And every customer, including this one, seems to have an issue with something. Another Monday. Everything seems to go wrong on a Monday. Jim fiddles at some items in his apron while waiting for a response. When there is none, he asks, "Did you hear me?"

Jeremiah asks, "Where else can I put it?" holding a stapler and a flier.

Jim points to a corkboard of business cards and event fliers in the back corner near the soft drinks and beers. "Right over there," he states, the answer obvious.

Jeremiah says, "But no one ever goes over there. This is where everyone comes in and can see the flier."

"I know that, I know that," Jim attempts to sound appeasing, sensible. "But it's just not the place for these sorts of things." The blue apron hung along his torso is dusted with white flour from pizza making, a few pens hang from various parts of it, and a box cutter and a telephone in the front pocket. Filling many roles in the small country store, he just wants Jeremiah to listen. He doesn't want a hard time.

"Listen, my son is missing, do you understand? It's been a year now. Please. All I'm asking is to put up a flier of him. That's all."

Jim listens, not because his heartstrings have been plucked or any such nonsense like that, but because he can sense from Jeremiah that this is the sort of man who isn't going to drop the issue. "Sure thing, buddy. I just ask that you purchase something." Jim figures that after the guy leaves, he can take the flier down anyway and avoid an argument. He walks back towards the register and sets the gas pump on with an apologetic wave through the window at the customer who has been patiently waiting at their car with a hand in the air to be noticed.

Jeremiah staples the flier up. While stuffing the small stapler back into his jeans, Jeremiah notices the pocket is vibrating. He pulls his phone out.

He expects it to be Bri, but the number to the police station is there on his screen. He pauses. Recent calls from the police have been with regards to complaints from people about Jeremiah. Jeremiah having put up fliers where they're not supposed to be. Jeremiah having been disorderly and unpleasant. Jeremiah needing to permit the police to do their job. Jeremiah answers, ready for another idle scolding, "Yes?"

"Is this Mr. Fray?"

"Yes." Jeremiah walks to the corkboard after deciding to put a flier up there anyway. It can't hurt. The phone is pinned between his shoulder and ear as he staples a flier over a grouping of business cards. He then returns to the front window. He only has one more flier, and he may as well tape one up there too.

"Mr. Jeremiah Fray, who reported his son missing, a Cole Fray?"

"Yes."

"Mr. Fray, we need you to come down to the station."

The breath of his dead question can be felt passing over his tongue and through his teeth as Jeremiah asks, "Why?"

"Mr. Fray, we believe we found your son. We need you to identify the body."

Jeremiah's arms sink to his sides. Stapler and flier in his hands. His heart stops. He stares out at the pumps and the bushes and the road and the trees. Cars driving. Clouds passing. He catches his own vague reflection. Only shards of him are visible among the papers and advertisements taped over the front window. He can see his shoulder, a hip, some of his right leg, and his eyes. He thinks it might be a faithful representation of how broken he is, as though an eraser were dragged across him, smudging pieces of his existence into a blur.

"Mr. Fray, are you still there?"

"Yes."

Jeremiah pictures himself having to tell Bri and Gavin and Abigail. He doesn't know what that will look like.

"Did you hear what I said, Mr. Fray? We believe we found your son and we need you to identify the body."

"Yes."

"I'm very sorry, sir, but it would be best if you could be here before 6:00pm."

"Okay."

31

Bri weeps. Bri weeps with everything in her as her body lies across the still body of her small son. Her back and arms shake atop her baby boy as she embraces him with her sobs, touches him, apologizes and tells him all about her love for him. The boy lies there unmoving as the crying of his mother overlays his cool pale skin.

Jeremiah stands just behind his wife, wanting to comfort her, to go near her, wanting to hold his son, press him to his body and say goodbye and kiss him. Instead, Jeremiah puts his hands into his pockets and steps out of the room. The metal door clicks shut behind him. An office. Computers. Half-filled mugs of cold coffee. The muffled sobs of his wife can still be heard behind him. Walking up to the officer who escorted them to the room, Jeremiah asks, "Where was my son found?" as though he might be talking about a lawn chair blown away.

The officer asks, "What's that?" while drawing his eyes up from the computer.

"Where was my son found?"

"Sure, let me look through the notes," the officer replies. He opens up a different program on the computer screen with forms and reports, scanning through updates. He opens up another folder, reviewing similar information. He says, "Yes sir, looks like he was found over off of Louisburg Road. If I know the area correctly, which I do," he explains, "I live right near there, nice new townhome my wife and I bought a few months ago." He catches himself. Scans the details. Professional voice. Somber. "The place your boy was found looks to be right near where they are building that new walking bridge. You know where I'm talking about, the one near that marsh?"

Jeremiah's mind has only picked up fragments of words, and he realizes a question has been asked as the officer looks at him. The question echoes in his mind. He pictures the newly constructed bridge that Gavin always points out as a place they'll need to walk soon so they can explore and find turtles and frogs.

Jeremiah answers, "Yes."

The officer announces, "He was found this morning by," he scans, "Officer Farag."

Jeremiah nods. He walks back out to where his son and wife are. The door clicks behind him. Returning to his wife, Jeremiah still refuses to look directly at his son, seeing only glimpses of him from the edges of his eyes as though afraid of his presence. Afraid of it being true. Cole's little toes are just barely in the corner of his vision as they stick up, unprotected in the air. Jeremiah wants to put socks on his son's feet to keep him from being cold.

Bri turns and presses herself to Jeremiah's chest. She wraps her arms around him as she quietly cries her son's name. Jeremiah holds Bri close. He begins to cry too, face to her hair. Jeremiah then grips the shoulders of his wife to show that he wants to walk to their son. Before he does, he brushes a tear from her face.

Jeremiah goes to Cole. He stands beside his returned son with his hands set on the metal table. The breath in his lungs is difficult. His shoulders heavy. His arms unreliable. Jeremiah turns his eyes to the bottom end of the table where Cole's bare feet are plastered in mud. He reaches out to touch the bare toes. The mud is hard and crisp. He flicks some away. The flesh beneath is cold. Jeremiah scans his eyes over Cole's legs and knees, thinned away, pale and starved. There are welts on his thighs. Cole's shorts are also covered in mud, and the smell of urine is strong. Cole had been doing so well with potty training, and the thought makes Jeremiah sick as he imagines Cole soiling himself against some wall. He looks at the shirt, Spider-Man valiantly swinging to save, and then up to his son's neck and face. The shirt has been ripped down at the collar. There are intense, mottled bruises splotched out over the boy's upper chest. Along Cole's neck is the evidence of strangulation. Cole's eyes are puffy and closed. Sad. Pained. His dirty face displays the paths of streamed away tears long dried out.

Jeremiah runs a hand up and down his son's arm as if to warm him. He announces softly, "I'm so sorry. My baby boy." His jaw quivers. Jeremiah's fingers go to his son's small hand and he clasps it in his. He kisses the hand. He kisses his son's lips. He kisses them again, brushing fingers through his son's hair. Jeremiah lays his face over Cole's neck as he hugs his baby boy, raising him from the table and swaying in mild rhythm. "I'm so sorry. My baby boy. I'm so sorry."

He rests Cole's body back to the table.

He kisses his son one last time. Touches his hair.

Before Jeremiah even really knows what he's doing, he's walking away from his son and past his wife who briefly reaches for him. Waves of pain and anger. Coursing.

The door swings closed behind him. Metal click. The officer orients himself back to Jeremiah, the chair squeaking with his attentive turn. The officer appears peevish. Six o'clock has passed.

Standing across from the officer's desk, Jeremiah asks, "Was my son beaten?"

The officer answers with hesitation, "Yes, sir. The bruising would indicate such."

"Was my son raped?"

A pause. The officer scratches at his chin. He answers, "Yes, that was also determined."

"My son was strangled to death? In some water and mud?"

"Yes, sir."

"Do you think my son cried?" The waves inside Jeremiah toss with fervor as his chest tremors with their frenzy.

The officer offers, "Sir, I think we should stop."

"Do you think my son cried?" Jeremiah yells.

"Sir, that's enough." The officer stands.

"Do you think my son cried? Do you think he cried for us to come to him? Do you think he expected us to save him that entire time he was missing? Where were you? None of you did a thing! None of you did a thing!"

"Sir that's enough, let's go ahead and go outside." The officer guides Jeremiah by the shoulder as he walks around the desk to provide escort.

Jeremiah shoves the officer, slamming him against the wall. Pictures and certificates crash down unhinged and shattering onto the floor.

Jeremiah punches the officer once, twice, again. The officer drops to deflect and hide as Jeremiah continues. Jeremiah then turns around. Reaching out, he slides his arms over the desk, flinging papers and smashing the computer to the ground as he does. A chair is kicked over and the desk flipped to the ground, and before Jeremiah knows it, he's on the floor, face slammed to the linoleum with his arms stretched behind his back in pain, a knee in his spine and cuffs on his wrists, shoulders wrenched. Jeremiah curses and screams. He can hear his wife crying in the background, begging for him to stop, as Jeremiah struggles in weeping rage on the ground.

Part Six

32

The funeral day is bright. Wispy clouds travel the thin blue sky at a playful pace. Delicate winds brush the trees as birds dance from branch to branch, teasing each other. They chirp, they sing. The buds of new leaves and flowers are beginning, awaking yet again for the season with promises of warmth. Spring, alive and tall, is shaking off her heavy winter layers to remind those around her of her stunning beauty.

The graveyard grounds are well-kept and green, as the deceased are provided the honor and care due them, with bright flowers laid near their gravestones, decorating their names and the years they lived. Blue canopied tents are set up in various spots throughout the graveyard in preparation for the funeral ceremonies scheduled today. There will be three. Beneath one of them, Jeremiah holds Gavin on his lap as he stares at the tiny casket where Cole lies. His legs are stiff. Lips dry. Bri sits to his right. Her kerchief goes to her eyes often. Abigail drapes herself over her mother's shoulder. The small girl is sleeping. Langdon sits to Jeremiah's left. His strong chest trembles with his restrained sobs, head sunk down in grief. Jeremiah finds himself rubbing his brow often with the heel of his hand, as though there might be some lump in his mind that must be flattened out, a nervous sort of thing. New to him.

From the podium, Pastor McDaniel offers comforting words to those gathered. He lifts up calls to God above for a new day and a new creation, where there will be no more death or tears or pain. He pauses throughout to regain his breaking voice. He wipes his eyes often.

There are subdued sobs all around as the memorial service continues. The air is decorated with the somber notes which are carried away by the spring breeze. Gavin doesn't cry. He seems to be watching it all, mesmerized by the novelty of such a thing so strange to him that he seems confused on how to be, especially as he sits atop the lap of his blank father. Jeremiah hates himself for that. He wants Gavin to be okay. Wants him to know it's okay to cry. He hopes he isn't ruining him.

Pastor's eyes are on Jeremiah in a hush, and Jeremiah realizes that everyone is waiting for him. It's his turn to speak.

Jeremiah stands from his chair and attempts to place Gavin back behind him in the seat, but the boy's arms reach for his father, not wanting to be left alone. Jeremiah assures his son that he'll be right back, but Gavin shakes his head, and Jeremiah has him in his arms again just to avoid a scene. Jeremiah walks to the podium. He presents himself to the many faces who have come to support and grieve. Rows and columns of people. Cole is before them all, lying within his casket. Jeremiah can still see the bruises there, the brutality. He imagines Cole squirming in the mud. Gasping. Crying. Dying. Jeremiah looks up.

Jeremiah goes to speak, but his voice dries out. He coughs. Attempts again, still unable. A few ladies in the aisle before him sigh at his sadness. He hates them for it. One woman gestures something with her lips about how *it's going to be alright.* He hates her more than anything.

"My son, Cole." He hesitates. "I loved him. Loved him with all my heart. We loved him," Jeremiah corrects, then says, "When Cole was an infant, people would ask Bri and I how old our baby girl was because of how fair Cole was. He was a beautiful baby. We could have dressed Cole in blue and put a construction helmet on his head and I swear people would have still asked us about our pretty baby girl. He was all boy though. We called him Cole-zilla because he always destroyed things, especially things that Gavin would build. He was a clunker, falling down and getting boo-boos constantly. He must have knocked his head on something at least three times a day. He'd always walk backwards while talking to you and hit his head on the corner of a wall or a doorknob, and then he'd do it again a few minutes later. He loved to wrestle. He loved doing cartwheels and handstands. He loved being held. He loved the

Darth Vader song for some reason. I was never a Star Wars fan, and he never watched the movies, so I have no idea how he even learned about it. If I didn't play the song for him, he would sing it. 'Bom bom bom, bom-bom-bom, bom-bom-bom.' There was this one time I told him I would never play it again, and he started crying. I was only kidding. I never should have said that. I should have just played it for him."

People smirk kindly in the crowd, grinning at his story. His eyes darken on them, but they don't seem to notice.

Jeremiah continues, "As an infant, he would smile at me, even though he didn't smile for anyone else. He smiled for me. I don't know why. I'd walk by him when he was on the floor or peek at him in his crib, and he'd see me and smile a little infant toothless smile. So beautiful. My beautiful son. It was hard though. A part of me was scared for a while that if I showed Cole too much affection that I would hurt my relationship with Gavin. I didn't know how to love two children at once. Not at first. I thought my heart was made of pieces, and I had to try and make sure that all the pieces were properly given out, and the more I gave the less I had. But that wasn't true. It took time to understand that I could love each of my children with all of my heart. And my wife too. Sometimes Cole would smile at me as an infant, and I didn't smile back."

Tears reach for his eyes. He waits a minute or so. He breathes. The people dressed in black wait patiently, and Jeremiah isn't sure why.

"Cole got bigger and he grew into his person. He was such a loving boy, so full of emotion. He would cry at movies. He would cry for other children when they were hurt. He was kind and sweet and sensitive. He either loved something or hated it. He either laughed or cried. If he wasn't yelling, he was whispering. He always said 'What?' That could be so annoying. You'd tell him something, and he would say 'What?' without even listening to what you said in the first place. There was this one time when Gavin broke one of Cole's toys. I told Gavin to apologize to Cole, and he did. Gavin said, 'Cole, please forgive me for breaking your toy.' Cole asked, 'What?' And Gavin said it again. 'Cole, please forgive me for breaking your toy.' Cole said again, 'What?' Gavin got upset. Gavin said it one last time, and Cole said again, 'What?'" Jeremiah smirks with the memory, staring at the podium. He can feel Gavin wriggling in his arms, uncomfortable with being talked about in front of so many people.

"I always thought I'd see Cole get old. I was hoping to get to know him as the man he'd be. He would have been a good man. Far better than me. I miss him, my baby boy. We all miss him. My baby boy, Cole. This never should have happened. I should have kept him with me in that store. I knew I shouldn't have left him. I should have kept him with me. I don't know why I didn't. It's not like me. I should have kept him with me." He stares at the casket. "When Bri and I saw Cole at the coroner, he was covered in mud and bruises. I don't know who took him, but whoever did, they abused our son. Brutalized our baby boy. Strangled him in some grass and mud and water."

The waves lick at his ribs, pulling and pushing and pulling against him, but Gavin has tensed in the telling of his brother's end, and Jeremiah holds his tongue as though realizing where he is. He looks over the people who appear off guard, as though this weren't the sort of funeral to which they're accustomed and he finishes, head up, "My son has died, and the world doesn't care."

Instead of returning to his place beside his wife who waits for him, Jeremiah walks away with Gavin. They go to a nearby pond off the edge of the parking lot. He asks his son if he wants to throw rocks in the water and the boy asks somberly, "Like we used to do with Cole?"

"Yes."

They throw rocks, skipping them across the surface. Gavin comments on throws Cole would have liked and Jeremiah can only nod as he considers the end of it all and how quickly it came, now passing behind them with another day half done. Holding a smooth flat stone, Jeremiah skips it, disrupting the pond with ripples as dragonflies scatter the air.

33

It's near midnight. The saddened home lies quiet as the family rests within their beds in coverings of grief. Soft breaths of sleep are in each room where the walls have lowered their eyes to the crying they have heard and witnessed.

Jeremiah tosses awake, lying on his side. His face is worn ragged with emotion spent, deep shadows cutting over his face in wrinkles that show the mortality consumed from him, a toll of passage paid early.

His burning eyes glimpse the slow opening of his bedroom door as it tilts. The weak glow of the boy's nightlight stretches thinly across the floor. Jeremiah wants to drop back to sleep and forget all of life, sleep away till his days are gone, but he glances towards the door while sitting up. A small figure of silhouette is in the open doorway with a blanket draped down from face to small feet. The boy waits, as if questioning whether or not he's welcome inside.

"Papa."

Jeremiah questions life and dreams and everything in between as he asks in a whisper, "Cole?"

"Papa."

Jeremiah goes to him, drawing his young son up into his arms. The boy wraps his arms around his father's neck, and Jeremiah sways, his face nuzzled against his son's neck to take in the sweet smells there.

"I miss you so much, Cole."

The boy relaxes, his body melting in the safety of his father.

"I'm sorry, Cole."

"It's okay, Papa."

"Stay with me," Jeremiah begs.

"Okay."

Jeremiah walks to the young boy's bedroom. He makes his way soundlessly beside the bunkbed and kneels down. Gavin remains asleep in the top bunk. Jeremiah lays Cole in his own bed.

"I'm cold, Papa," Cole says as he nestles his head into his pillow.

Jeremiah draws the comforter up towards the boy's chin. "Is that better?"

Cole shuffles in the sheets and blankets. "Yes." His eyes shut.

Jeremiah brushes his fingers over his son's face, wishing above all, wishing to just hold his real son alive again, wishing this is how it could have always been and always would be.

Jeremiah whispers near his son's ear, "I love you, Cole."

But Cole has become still and motionless, his chest unmoving within the folds of his bed. Kissing his son's cheek, the skin is now cold and dry, tasting of dirt and pain and tears. Purple marks cover the boy's neck. Jeremiah rests his face atop Cole's body, crying there against his son.

"I'm so sorry, Cole. I'm so sorry."

34

There are a few knocks at the front door. Gavin goes and opens it to Pastor McDaniel who is waving down at the young boy through the window. The porch light decorates his smiling face. Moths and other tiny nighttime bugs fly in the light.

"Why, hello, Gavin," Pastor greets while ducking his head unnecessarily in the entrance as he steps through.

"Why are you here?" Gavin asks.

"I'm here to talk to your Papa," Pastor answers with a grin.

"About Cole?"

"Sort of."

"Cole is in heaven. That's what Mommy said," Gavin says.

Pastor crouches down and wraps Gavin in his long arms. "Yes he is." He squeezes Gavin tightly.

Pastor states, "It's a surprisingly chilly evening for April," and with that, Gavin releases Pastor, as though not old enough to talk about the weather just yet. Gavin goes into the kitchen, asking for Fruit Snacks from his mother. A moment later, Bri comes out with Gavin at her side as the boy opens the small pack and she says, "Thank you for coming." She offers Pastor a hug.

"Of course," he says.

Bri ushers Gavin upstairs to put him to bed, telling him to finish up the fruit snacks so he can brush his teeth. The living room is vacated. Pastor is left alone, waiting. He unwraps his scarf from around his neck and takes his cap off, stuffing it into his brown coat pocket. He drapes the coat over the arm of the couch. He then rubs his hands together as though to warm them. As though nervous.

A moment later Jeremiah says, "Pastor," while coming down the stairs in measured pace. Pastor smiles and they shake hands as they meet together in the center of the room. After the greeting, Jeremiah sits in a chair. Jeremiah knows why Pastor is here, knows that Bri must have called him over to talk because she doesn't know what else to do. Jeremiah wants to be angry with that, but knows he's left her little choice.

"Do you mind if I sit down?" Pastor asks.

"Not at all." Jeremiah shakes his head, trying to remember himself and his manners. He brushes his hair out of his eyes, forcing strands to the side that momentarily rest at the edge of his eyebrow. He rubs his palm there up and down, left and right. It's raw. Hand to his lap, the strands of hair drop back across his vision and this time he leaves it that way. He scratches his arm. Crosses his legs. Rubs his brow again. Scratches his arm feverishly as though bugs were there. He is suddenly confronted by where he is and the instability of his mind as it seeps its way out into his person, and he wonders how he might look to others, knowing he hardly resembles who he always was. Even his tone and mannerisms seem to have changed. More harsh. People have been avoiding him, tossing their eyes away. But he's encouraged that, avoiding everyone he can as he has crept away into the cave of his person. He feels as though little remains of him. Like clinging leaves from a long dead tree. Like ruined feathers of a skeleton bird.

"How are you?" Pastor asks.

Jeremiah looks at him. Such a strange question. "I don't know."

"People are worried about you, Jeremiah."

"They shouldn't be."

Pastor restates, "Bri is worried about you. And Langdon."

"I know." Jeremiah watches his fingers as they drum atop the cushion.

Pastor admits, "I came to talk."

"I know."

"Would you like to talk?"

"I don't know. Not really."

Pastor offers with sympathy, "Do you think it would help?"

Jeremiah considers. "I don't even know what that means."

Pastor offers, "Sometimes talking can help."

"You mean we could talk about what happened?"

"If that's what you'd like, sure."

"No. I wouldn't."

Pastor grins in an attempt to lighten the air and says, "People say you're not so nice anymore."

Jeremiah asks, "What do you tell them?"

"I tell them they must not know you very well because you were never too nice in the first place." Pastor smiles.

Jeremiah almost smirks, but it goes away. He asks in a sarcastic challenge, "Are you going to tell me there might be some sin I need to repent of, and that's the reason for what happened to Cole?"

Pastor McDaniel assures, "Of course not, Jeremiah."

"Did they tell you what happened?"

Pastor nods. "Yes."

"Did they tell you how much repentance I needed to offer for all the horrible things I said to them?"

"They did."

"What'd you say?"

"That's not much of your business, Jeremiah, sorry." Pastor McDaniel grins.

"Did you tell them to shut-up in the name of Jesus?"

Pastor smiles. "Something like that."

"I wanted to hurt them for what they said."

Pastor assures, "I'm sure you did. I would too."

"I think the only reason I didn't hurt them was because I knew Gavin was watching."

"Then I'm glad Gavin was there."

"It hurt Bri. When they said that." Jeremiah looks away, sad.

"I'm sure. I'm sorry."

"That's what got me so angry. Not that it hurt me. I didn't care about that. But it hurt Bri."

"I know."

Jeremiah scratches his arm again, like a dog with fleas. He looks away, wanting to move on and move away.

"How is everyone, Jeremiah?"

"We're struggling. Bri is strong, much stronger than me. She's strong for Gavin and for Abigail, holding everything together because I can't. I don't mean to be so selfish, you know. But I'm wearing on her. I wake up sometimes and tell myself I'll start today, start being better. And then I'm not."

"You will be."

Jeremiah ignores that. "Bri cries a lot at night, when she thinks I'm sleeping. She used to hold me when she did, but now she doesn't. Abigail doesn't understand. But she knows something's wrong. She points at pictures of Cole and says, 'Cozy!' Gavin is hurting. He sees me not cry and he thinks that's how he should be. I tell him it's okay, it's okay to cry. I tell him not to be like me. He needs to grieve. To let it out."

"So do you."

"I don't."

"Why not? Are you so strong?" Pastor challenges.

"It's not that at all." Jeremiah states, "I don't deserve to."

Pastor tilts his head with a grimace. "That's foolish, Jeremiah."

"Is it?"

"Yes, it is."

"It's not."

"Jeremiah."

"Don't say it again. Don't."

Pastor's lips seal away any words. Then he says, "You need to permit healing, Jeremiah, for you and for your family. You must move on."

"I won't."

"Look at what it's doing to you. To your family."

Jeremiah nods in agreement. He acknowledges, "I've turned into someone who is short-tempered and mean. I snap at everything, and I'm stuck not knowing what to do. I make Abigail cry. I make Bri cry." Jeremiah apprehends the simplicity of it all. "I make everyone cry. I'm destroying everyone I love, and I don't know what else to do. I don't know what to do."

Pastor asks, "Then why not try to be there for them?"

"I don't remember how."

Pastor McDaniel is suddenly made aware of his ineptitude as he finds a comforting word elusive, as something only believed upon during easier days and for simpler difficulties. He simply says, "I'm sorry."

"It's okay."

"It's not."

"It is."

"I want you to know that I have no false notions of understanding what you're going through, Jeremiah."

"It's okay."

Seeing Jeremiah's walls rising, Pastor asks, "Do you still pray?"

Jeremiah blinks. Hatred there. "When Cole was first taken, I begged God, begged him with all of my tears and with every strand of who I am, begged him to bring Cole back. Day in and day out, I begged God to help me find my son. I fully believed he would. A grain of mustard seed, you know. Then, after months with no answer, I blamed God for not stopping it in the first place. For not bringing Cole back. I blamed him for it all. I stopped praying because I hoped it would hurt him. But then I started looking around at the people in this world, how little they care. How small their hearts are. I began to see that it is men who make this world so vile. Not God. Men rape. They molest. They kidnap. They murder. They pervert. Even if people blame God for the bad things that happen, it is men who do horrible things to each other. To children. It is men who make this earth so gross. People blame God, but they're silly for doing so." He stops and smiles. "*Silly*. That's a funny time to use such a word. It's a *silly* time to use such a word." He laughs.

Pastor pauses, unsure of the soundness sitting across from him, but he beckons for Jeremiah to continue.

Jeremiah says, "So, God didn't answer, and that's okay. I don't blame Him anymore. I blame myself. I blame the man who did it. I blame the man who beat my son with fists, who raped and molested my boy, who strangled him in shallow water." His chest tightens, shortening his breath and his words. "I blame him for stealing everything from me and my family. He robbed me of every good memory I had of my son. I am plagued now, infected in my mind." He grabs his skull by the fingertips and squeezes as if to extract some sickness. His eyes bulge. "I dream of us together again. Then I wake up and we're not. I dreamt last night that Cole was at the front door knocking. I could see his blue eyes smiling at me through the window. I can't explain the joy I felt. There was this sudden sense that everything we'd been through, all the pain and sadness, that those things had been a dream, a long drawn-out nightmare. And there he was, Cole, back home. I ran to the door, but when I opened it, he wasn't there. And I woke up. I think constantly about how much he must have cried. About how much he must have suffered. How alone he was." Jeremiah takes a moment to breathe, the fervor of his words have exhausted him. Between the shortened gasps, he says as best as he can, "God is a God of justice. I believe that. I want God to send whoever did this to hell. I want him there now, and I want to hear him scream."

Pastor says, "Jeremiah, that's not your place. That's not what we're called to be. We are called to wait for God's justice."

Jeremiah squints. "Yeah."

"Jeremiah."

"I'm not good enough for that."

"It's not about being good enough, Jeremiah. It's what we are called to be."

"Pastor." Jeremiah eyes Pastor McDaniel with stern disdain. "I don't care."

Instead of indulging the argument Jeremiah seems to desire, Pastor encourages, "Jeremiah, please close your eyes."

Jeremiah closes them. In the darkness, he scratches his arm and nose and scalp and arm.

Pastor offers, "Jeremiah, give that anger, that rage, that sense of justice that you crave, give it to Christ. He can heal you. He alone. Give it to Him, offer it to Him, and He can both remain pure and make you clean, washing you with His loving hands. He cares for you. He loves you. He always has. He always will. Jeremiah, let the bitterness and rage drop off of you. Let it slide away. Leave it on the ground behind you as you walk on. You don't need it anymore. Your family needs you to let it go. Do it for them. In that release, find those memories of Cole as he always was, remember him with fondness, with the love of a father. After giving it all to Christ, you stand. You stand anew, clean and released of your hatred, your bitterness, and your hurt. You have peace knowing that Christ will make things right, and that Cole is with Him. And you will be with him again. You are cleansed and made free. You are able to be there for Bri and Gavin and Abigail again. You can be the father and husband they need you to be. The father and husband you want to be." Pastor concludes, "Keep your eyes closed, Jeremiah. Tell me what you see."

Jeremiah imagines the front of their home. He's there, standing at the steps. Gavin, Bri, and Abigail are with him. He's with his family. Everyone is smiling. He's holding Bri's hand. Abigail is in his arms. Gavin holds his leg. Then the image of himself, his body, his face, his hair, dries and crisps to gray, and a breeze brushes pieces of him away in ashes that are drawn into the air along with all that he is. He's gone. His family remains. Then his family disappears too. The empty home is all that's left.

Pastor asks, "What do you see?"

"I see nothing."

Pastor yields in failure. Deep within, he's truly convinced that time will soften the grief in Jeremiah, because it always does. He's certain God will heal and draw Jeremiah with bands of love. He prays silently for protection and healing for the family.

Eyes still closed, Jeremiah admits, "Yesterday, I started praying again."

Pastor responds, sitting forward, "That's good," maybe thinking God has already heard and begun an answer. "That's good." He can't help the hopeful smile.

Jeremiah explains, "Now, when I pray, I bow my head and close my eyes. With every drop of blood in my tainted veins, I pray that God comes and burns this place. I pray He burns this earth and everything in it to ash, and I beg Him to start with me."

35

A knock. Jeremiah stands and walks to the front door, thinking how all he seems to do now is open the front door to people who want to visit and check in on the family. Offer condolences. Encouragements. Then they leave. Jeremiah opens the door. "Langdon." He's embarrassed by the sight of his friend standing before him as he recalls every moment he's refused to answer the phone or respond to Langdon's attempts at reaching him.

Langdon's clear blue eyes are intense. He asks, "Can I come in?" The uncertainty of his tone fills Jeremiah with guilt.

"Of course." Jeremiah steps aside.

They avoid any touch as Langdon passes inside. Langdon goes to sit on the couch. He anticipates Jeremiah sitting across from him like they always used to during conversations that seemed to fill an afternoon or an evening, but Jeremiah walks to the wall where the window blinds are drawn open. He stares outside.

Langdon gathers in a sense of Jeremiah to know how best to speak to him. He won't remove his eyes from Jeremiah, as though a piece of his friend might be brought back and he's searching on how to find him. He asks, "Where is everyone?"

"Bri took Gavin and Abigail to the store or something."

"You didn't want to go?"

"Not really."

Langdon asks, "How is everyone?"

"We're fine. We're healing. We're getting along okay. Now we can move on," Jeremiah lies. It's his new favorite phrase. People like to nod at such a thing. Jeremiah looks through the window as he leans against the wall, watching children play tag. They duck their shoulders and run with shrieks of glee.

"Stop pretending that I'm like everyone else," Langdon says. "I don't deserve that."

"I know. I'm sorry."

Langdon asks, "Have you been avoiding me?"

"No," Jeremiah answers, his back still to Langdon.

"Then why don't you answer my phone calls?"

"I don't know."

Langdon states, "Try me."

It takes Jeremiah a moment to admit, "Because I'd want to talk."

Langdon asks, "Why is that bad?"

"Because I'd probably just start crying."

"There's nothing wrong with that."

"But I'm so tired of crying."

"Do you think I've cried? Do you think I've cried over Cole?" Langdon challenges.

Jeremiah states, "I don't know."

Langdon stops himself from saying some of the harsher things he'd like to, his hands clasped together in tightening fists. He says, "Of course I have. Day after day."

Jeremiah offers, "I'm sorry. I know you have. I don't mean to be so cold."

"I know."

Jeremiah admits, "I miss him. Cole."

"I know."

Rubbing his brow, Jeremiah feels dizzy, like a child spun in the air long after it's no longer fun. He's unsure of his own thoughts and beliefs as they toss around in his head, as if everything he's been told must be looked at now with uncertainty. The ground beneath his feet, once believed solid, is now soft and sinking.

A part of him wants to tell Langdon more.

A part of him wishes Langdon never came.

Langdon asks, "So, what now?"

Running his fingertips up and down the blinds rhythmically, Jeremiah answers, "If it wasn't for my family, I'd blow my brains out." He stops his fingers in anticipation of the expected reproof.

"Or," Langdon offers, "you could hang yourself."

"There are options," Jeremiah agrees.

"Maybe just pills, if you're feeling womanly."

"I do feel like a woman lately."

"You were always in touch with your feminine side."

"I know, right?" Jeremiah almost grins.

Jeremiah strums his fingers over the blinds again. The short-lived banter is gone.

Langdon clarifies, "Don't blow your brains out. I was only kidding."

Jeremiah grins at the wall. "I know." He says, "This morning, Gavin tried to show me something he built with Legos. I glanced at it. It was great. He's getting so good at building. So creative. I wanted to tell him it was wonderful. I wanted to hold him. But I walked past him like a phantom. I've been cold to him, and he's avoided me lately. I'm sorry for that. He stays in his room a lot. I should have thought more about how Gavin was affected by Cole. Do you know at all what I mean?"

Langdon offers, "Yes."

Jeremiah nods.

Langdon asks, "So, why not now?"

"What do you mean?"

Langdon asks, "Why not be there for Gavin now?"

"Maybe that's what I'll do."

"I'm being serious."

Jeremiah assures, "Me too."

"Okay, good." Langdon sits more upright. He asks, "How's Bri?"

Jeremiah shakes his head. "She's gotten the worst of me."

Langdon corrects, "She always has."

Jeremiah smirks at that. It saddens him as well. "I know. But I don't want to see her. I can't help her with her sadness."

"Maybe you should try."

"It's a burden I can't bear. She wants to grieve together. She wants to heal. She knows Cole is gone and we can't change that. She talks about him being in heaven, and I believe he is, but all I can think about is how he looked on that table and the things that were done to him. That's all I see when I close my eyes. I can't move on. Not yet."

"Why not?"

"Why not, what?"

"Why can't you move on?"

"It would mean forgetting what has happened. It would feel like I was betraying Cole. Like I was failing him again."

"It doesn't have to mean that."

Jeremiah's lip quivers. He says nothing.

Langdon asks with gentle challenge, "So, what are you going to do? You won't move on. You won't be there for your wife and children. So, what are you going to do? Hide in your house all day and get old?"

"You make me sound like a loser."

"Maybe you are."

Jeremiah smirks. Langdon untying him.

Langdon asks again, seeking deeper, "What's next, Jeremiah? What are you going to do?"

Jeremiah states, "I need to find him." He leaves no question of whom he's speaking.

"Why?"

Jeremiah's responds in a flare of anger, "Are you kidding me?"

"No. I'm not."

"You know why," Jeremiah says.

"Then say it."

"No."

"Say it."

"I don't want to."

"Why not?"

"I don't want to."

"Why not, Jeremiah?"

"Fine. I'd kill him."

"And then what?"

"Cut him into pieces."

"That not what I meant."

"Then what do you mean, Langdon?"

"Don't you think I want the same? I think about it all the time, you know, what I'd do to whoever killed Cole. I even imagine doing it for you so that you wouldn't go to prison and you wouldn't ever have to let that part of you out."

"Which part is that?" Jeremiah asks.

"You know which part."

Nothing else is said.

"Jeremiah?" Langdon asks.

"Yeah?"

"If you do something to the man who did this, you'll go to prison. And if you do it the way you'd want, you'd probably go to prison for life."

"I know. But if I don't –"

"I understand. But you have a family. That's what I want you to remember. And I hate to say it, Jeremiah, but Cole is gone. He isn't hurting anymore."

"I am," Jeremiah confesses. He hates how selfish it sounds.

"I know." Langdon warns again, "If you go to prison, you'll be taken from your family, and I don't want that for you, or for them. You don't want that."

Jeremiah's head sinks. "I know."

"I just want to remind you. I love you. I'm your friend, and whatever happens, I'll still love you and be your friend. And if you go to prison, I'll even sneak in steak for you like we used to do for Tim. But I don't want you in prison. I want you here. I want you here with your family. And with me."

Jeremiah says, "I want that too. Trust me, I don't want to watch my wife and children get old from behind bars. Even thinking about it hurts. But what else do I do?"

"You cry. You spend time with your family. You heal with them. You play with Gavin. You hold Abigail. You spend time with Bri. You answer my phone calls and hang out with me."

"I can't do those things."

"Why not?" Langdon pleads.

Jeremiah bursts out, "I already told you! Why can't anyone understand?"

Langdon presses, "Are you ready to go to prison, Jeremiah? Are you ready to leave your family?"

Jeremiah's words are tight and terse. "The man who did this deserves something horrible! For everything he did to Cole!"

"I agree. But I'm asking if you would be willing to go to prison. That's reality."

Jeremiah's anger fades. "Maybe. No. I don't know. I don't know anything anymore. Sometimes that's the worst part. I don't know. I don't know what to do or how to be. When I think about my wife and children visiting me in prison, it breaks my heart. I'm ashamed. But when I imagine going my whole life pretending it's all over and moving on, I feel like a coward."

"It doesn't make you a coward. And it doesn't mean you have to pretend."

Jeremiah ignores that. "Sometimes, I imagine Gavin and Abigail as adults. I imagine them asking me, 'Papa, did you ever think about going after the man who raped and murdered Cole?' But I'll just be some old pathetic coward with some old pathetic coward excuse like, 'Well, that wasn't my place,' or 'I thought of you two angels,' or 'God wouldn't want that.' And I can hear them saying something back, something like, 'but Papa, that man strangled Cole and beat him and raped him. Shouldn't you have done something?'" Jeremiah twists the blinds open and closed, open and closed, the veins of his arms pulsing with distress.

Langdon offers, "They wouldn't say that."

"They should."

"They shouldn't, they won't."

"They should," Jeremiah restates.

"Does Bri know what you're thinking?"

Jeremiah admits, "No. She'd just tell me not to think such awful things. She'd tell me to be at home with my children and with her and to let the police find the man." He stops turning the blinds. "She'd say she doesn't want to lose me."

"She loves you."

"She shouldn't."

"That's stupid, Jeremiah."

"I'm sorry. You're right. I love Bri. With all my heart."

"I know."

Jeremiah admits, "It's never going to happen though."

"What's that?"

"All this daydreaming about vengeance. My obsessing. I'm just going to get old. That's how life is."

"Maybe that's a good thing."

"Maybe." Jeremiah asks, "Langdon?"

"Yeah?"

"Thanks for everything."

Langdon states, "I haven't done anything."

"You did. You have. More than you know."

"I could have done more."

Jeremiah confesses, "I don't think it would have changed anything."

"It might have."

"I'm not sure. But you were there. You were my friend."

"I still am."

"I know. Langdon?"

"Yeah?"

"Do you think Jeffrey Dahmer is in heaven?"

"I do."

"Even after all the grotesque things he did?"

"Yes."

"Have you ever looked at the horrible pictures of his victims? The severed heads and the body parts?"

"Yes."

"Me too."

"I know."

"And even after looking at them, you still think he's in heaven."

"I do."

"Most people wouldn't think so."

"That's okay."

"Most people would say such an idea was disgusting."

"I know."

"If I did it. If I killed the man who murdered Cole, do you think God would forgive me?"

"I believe Christ can forgive all sins."

"I don't know anymore."

"He can. He does."

"I left Cole in that store, Langdon. I lost my own son." Jeremiah begins to tremble and cry. "It's all my fault. And I loved him so much."

Langdon goes to Jeremiah. He pulls him into his arms. With his fists gripping tight to Langdon's shirt, Jeremiah sobs in the arms of his friend.

36

Something is on the radio. Words and things. Jeremiah isn't sure if he turned it on as he sits on the couch thinking and considering things that pass through his mind. He wishes the radio was off. But he doesn't feel like standing. The voices debate over sports. Nothing ever sounded so pointless.

He can feel the passing of time and it's effect upon him. The nightmares are less harsh. Less frequent. The echoes of Cole's crying are rarely heard, often in remnants that quickly vanish. The days are somehow softer. Good memories come to him. Remembrances of smiles and laughter that he had forgotten. Cole happy. Cole running and smiling. Cole in his arms. His baby boy with the day in his eyes. His baby boy talking to him. Despite trying to hold onto the bitterness, it has begun to evade him.

The police have had nothing on leads. Not that he really expected any. He only calls them every few days or so – not multiple times every day like he had been. The police have told him repeatedly that this is a matter for them, for the police, and to leave it in their capable hands. They said capable, and he had to hang up because he was laughing so hard. He truly hopes they find whoever did this to his son. He hopes the man serves time in prison.

Bri comes downstairs with Abigail in her arms, Gavin a few steps behind. Gavin shimmies past his mother and sits beside the bucket of shoes where he finds his boots and pulls them on. Abigail is bundled up with boots of her own and a polka-dot coat, and she pulls at the hood as something she doesn't want there, yanking it over her shoulder with irritation. Her dirty-blond hair has lengthened with curls at her shoulders. She seems to have a new word every day. So engaging and talkative, intelligence in her bright blue eyes. The tiny girl is growing in every way.

Bri stands beside the couch Jeremiah sits on as he stares at the wall. Abigail leans down from Bri as she tries to drop to her father. Jeremiah notices and looks up, ready for his daughter to turn away from him like she normally does, as though he were a stranger, as though he were a ghoul wandering the walls of the home. Instead, Abigail places an innocent and unlearned kiss onto her father's face with her arms around his head. The little lips placed upon Jeremiah disarm him. He looks up. He reaches for Abigail and pulls her close. The smells of tearless shampoo and baby powder bring flashes of his babies, loving every moment of their lives. "I love you, Abigail," he whispers in her ear. His bristles tickle her face and Abigail pushes against him, stretching away, but her eyes light up at seeing his eyes, as though he'd just returned, and she places another wide kiss on her father's mouth as though unable to resist. Holding her, Jeremiah's arms fatigue quickly, and he places Abigail back into Bri's care as he says, "I love you, Abigail."

Bri offers, "I'm going to take the kids out back and push them on the swing set."

Gavin announces, "Mom, I can do it by myself."

"Okay," Jeremiah says. He then adds, "It looks beautiful outside. What day is it?"

"Saturday."

"Okay. Good."

Bri asks with reservation, "Do you want to come out with us?"

"Not really. Not yet."

Bri offers, "You can't sit there your whole life, Jeremiah."

He agrees, "I know." He's thought this much lately, like an important task on his mind when first stirred from sleep. Like something he should get to soon.

"Papa, want to come out and watch me swing?" Gavin asks while yanking the back door open after unlocking the dead bolt with a grunt.

"I do," Jeremiah answers. He stands from the couch. Bri straightens tall with surprise. She smiles at her husband as he turns with a smile of his own. It tapers off, as though too heavy to hold up.

Fresh air greets them in the backyard, drawing the family further out, as if holding each hand. The warm sun lends energy to Jeremiah. The air in his lungs feels clean and good. He looks around as though everything was new.

Stepping off the deck, Jeremiah notices that the grass needs to be cut as it comes up higher than his ankles and he realizes that it's mid-May. Maybe after cutting the lawn, he'll shower and shave, and he runs his fingers through the thick beard covering his jaw as if just noticing he grew one.

Bri places Abigail into her plastic seat and buckles her in while Gavin takes off with legs kicking in timed rhythm to send him higher and higher. Jeremiah watches, hand on the wooden frame. He thinks he should call Emad soon and go back to work. He's still a father, a husband, and he needs to provide. Bills have accumulated on the kitchen table, despite Emad helping periodically. As he leans against the swing set he built with Langdon in preparation for Gavin's birth years ago, Jeremiah announces, "You're doing a great job, Gavin."

Jeremiah walks over to his wife. He stands behind her, placing his hands on her hips. Reaching over her shoulder, he kiss her cheek. The feel of her body and the smell of her hair, they stir his blood, and he offers in contrition, "I miss you."

"I miss you too," she says, turning her lips to him. They hold and kiss. Bri lays a palm on Jeremiah's cheek and then reaches behind his neck, thankful to have her husband returned. She wasn't sure if he'd ever come back. With no one to push her, Abigail's swings soon taper off, with her arms remaining out from her body with expectation of more pushes being provided. The little girl begins to screech as she kicks her legs, begging to be pushed again and looking side to side for why everything stopped. Jeremiah leaves the kiss with his wife and goes to his daughter. She shrieks happily again as he pushes her.

Gavin continues to fly up and down alongside them. As his hair tosses up and down with his swings, Gavin says, "Cole would say I'm going super high."

"Yes, he would," Jeremiah agrees while giving his daughter another push,

37

Gavin rests in the top bunk of the hushed bedroom. His blanket hangs from the edge of the bed, his arm dangling down. Jeremiah peeks in, but then turns away, not wanting to disturb his son. "Papa?" Gavin asks from the sheets.

Jeremiah walks to the bed. He runs his fingers through Gavin's hair as the boy breathes gently, tiredly. The boy yawns.

Gavin asks, "Papa, will you sing to me?"

"Of course."

Jeremiah restores their nighttime tradition held back from a time ago, rubbing his son's back while singing in whispers, *Itsy Bitsy Spider-Man* and *Jesus Loves Me*. Jeremiah always related his ungifted singing to the scratching caws of a crow, but Gavin never seemed to mind. The boy's breaths are soon smooth and deep. Jeremiah remains at his side, still brushing Gavin's back as Bri stands nearby in the open doorway, happy for the first signs of healing – thankful to God for the day her husband came back.

Part Seven

38

"Smell this," Jeremiah offers, lowering a clear bag of green unroasted coffee beans for Gavin to smell.

With a crinkling of his nose and a shake of his head, Gavin says, "Yuck, why do you like those?"

"I don't." Jeremiah then places a small Tupperware bowl of freshly roasted coffee beans to Gavin's nose, the aroma is rich and potent as it reaches out in boasting to the young boy. Jeremiah provides Gavin an opportunity to appreciate the contrast.

The boy's nose doesn't crinkle, but he remains unimpressed. However, he seems to understand a difference as he offers, "Yeah, those don't stink as bad."

Jeremiah smirks. "You're getting big, my boy."

"Yeah," Gavin agrees. "Someday, I'll be big like you."

Jeremiah squats down. With his index finger and thumb presented about three inches apart for Gavin to see, Jeremiah explains, "When you were born, you were just this little."

Gavin's eyes go wide. "I was?"

Jeremiah nods, fingers remaining apart for Gavin's continued marvel. "Yes. When you were that little I used to put you in my shirt pocket and carry you wherever I went. You'd peek your head out and I'd give you little cookies and you'd munch them and get crumbs everywhere. I didn't mind though. And I would show you off to everyone and tell them how proud I was to be your Papa. I would point at your tiny head poking out and say, 'this is my son, Gavin.' You'd look at them and just nibble at the cookie you had and toss crumbs everywhere."

Gavin's eyes glimmer as he says, "That's not true," but his father's piercing gaze causes him to ask, "is it?"

"It is."

"Papa, I want oatmeal for breakfast."

"I guess my story wasn't too exciting."

"I liked it." Looking up at his father, Gavin asks again, "Was I really that small?"

"Yep." Jeremiah smiles.

"I still don't think I was that small."

Jeremiah grins.

Jeremiah prepares the oatmeal, cutting fruit and starting the water on the stove. Gavin goes to sit at the table, spoon ready. Placing the steaming bowl in front of his son, Jeremiah offers a short prayer of thanks to which Gavin offers "amen" with a scoop full of oatmeal already in his mouth. Jeremiah sits at the table as he waits for Bri to come downstairs.

While looking at his father in the quiet morning of breakfast at the table and the beginning of the day, Gavin asks, "Papa, do you miss Cole?"

The massive bristling thorn that resides perpetually within Jeremiah's chest throbs in pain with its turning as it is stirred alive by Gavin's question. Jeremiah hides the pain as best he can. "Always."

Gavin says, "Me too."

Jeremiah says, "You're going to get older, and you're going to start to forget things."

Gavin looks up. "Why?"

"It's what we do."

"Who?"

"People."

"Oh."

Jeremiah says, "But you need to remember Cole. Even though he's gone, he'll always be your baby brother."

"How do I do that?"

"Well, what did you enjoy doing with him?"

Gavin looks at his bowl of oatmeal in contemplation. "I liked building things with him. And laughing. And playing Legos. And playing Angry Birds. And eating donuts."

Jeremiah smiles. "Good. Every time you do those things, you think of him. And as you get older, you tell Abigail about them, too. She didn't have the opportunity to know him like you did, so you'll need to tell her everything you can."

"Okay." Gavin considers. "But I probably won't have to tell you because you'll remember."

Jeremiah corrects, "No. I want you to tell me, too."

"In case you forget?"

"In case I forget. And because I like hearing them."

"Okay." Gavin smiles and nods, happy to do those things. He takes a bite of oatmeal and asks, "Is that what you do?"

"What?"

"Think about things you liked to do with Cole?"

"Sometimes. I need to do it more."

Gavin asks, "Because sometimes it's hard to remember?"

Jeremiah nods. "Yes. Sometimes it's hard to remember."

Bri comes downstairs. Bri and Jeremiah sit on the couch with their coffee. Abigail sits on her father's legs eating fistfuls of Cheerios from a bowl, most of them dropping to the couch and onto Jeremiah's lap. Jeremiah accepts the realization that this is what life will be from now on. This is how he must be as one called "father" and "husband." He sits on the couch, enjoying coffee with his wife, and he doesn't hate himself for it, not like he thought he would. Not like he wanted to. He almost cries, unsure why.

"Uncle Langdon is here! He has donuts!" Gavin calls out.

"Good." Jeremiah smiles. "Let him in."

Gavin hops from his seat and opens the door, smiling big with expectation as the vibrant sun pours over him. Uncle Langdon climbs the steps, bends down, and lifts Gavin into his arms.

39

Jeremiah fumbles at the gas pump for a moment before realizing in the dull and listless morning that it doesn't accept credit cards. He looks at the phone on his clock and grows anxious. He's pretty sure he'll be late for work, and he doesn't want that. He's made it through two weeks now of being back, and he wants to ensure there's no question about his ability to stay consistent. To keep it together. He wants to prove to Emad that he can be the dependable employee he always was.

When he returned to work on a Monday two weeks ago, the first thing he had to deal with were the countless questions from coworkers about how things turned out with Cole, along with hearing the condolences from their moving jaws. The second, and more difficult thing he had to deal with, was coming home. Not having Cole clomping down the driveway with his bowed legs while yelling "Papa!" Not having Cole declare something about his little day.

Abigail now comes down to greet him, ambling carefully down the slope of the asphalt on her new feet. She's spent most of the evenings in her father's arms, not wanting to be away from him. He's held her, and found strength there.

At the gas pump, Jeremiah flips through his wallet. No cash. The bells jingle above his head as he walks inside.

The lady behind the counter takes his credit card in a wrinkled hand and asks, "How much, darlin'?"

Jeremiah looks outside at his car as if he could tell by looking at it how much gas it might need and he answers, "Twenty, I guess."

"Twenty-dollars," she repeats while beeping some buttons and scanning his card through. She presents the card back, as well as the thin receipt paper for him to sign, and she asks, as if in awe of the scratched out scribble, "You a doctor or something?"

"No."

"That signature sure is something else." She peers at it.

"I'm just lazy, I guess."

She laughs at that – a big country gaffaw. She then slips the receipt through a slot in the register and tells him to have a blessed day, and he tells her to do the same.

The gas pump slows when it comes to about $18.50, even with a dollar and fifty to go, like a scrupulous, tight-eyed scrooge ensuring it doesn't dribble out a penny more. When finished, Jeremiah shakes the nozzle a few times within the tank and returns it to its place with a heavy drop down clank of metal on metal.

Putting the car in drive, Jeremiah edges away toward the main road, but the car rocks to a hard stop as his foot slams into the brake. He sits up, staring over the steering wheel. A woman climbs out from her dingy and dinged up white car. A young teenage boy stands from the passenger side and follows her toward the store.

The woman yells out, "Madge! Madge, I know you're in there! Come out, you old bag!"

A responsive rage burns Jeremiah's belly as the waves return from their idle departure, crashing insatiably in a crazed unrest within his skin as they toss his person with their mighty weight. Jeremiah waits, eyes unblinking.

40

Jeremiah trails the small white car, careful to stay back far enough to remain unnoticed, like some amateur private investigator. Back roads and trees and mailboxes. The white car eventually turns into a neighborhood where two story homes are painted in pastel and springtime colors. Fresh trees and new mulch. Some homes are still skeletal with their thin plywood walls and wooden frames, as the neighborhood continues to be built. Towards the end of the neighborhood, the woman and her son pull into their driveway and Jeremiah parks a few homes down along the curb of the street.

With bags of groceries in their arms, the mother and son walk into their home. They don't so much as glance in Jeremiah's direction. A few moments later, the boy returns for one last load and then shuts the trunk. Five plastic bags hang from his arms as he carries them in, and he boasts loud enough for Jeremiah to hear through the windshield, "Look how many I can carry, Mom!"

"You are my strong boy," the air carries her words from the open kitchen window, her thin face visible from behind the window box in bloom with white and purple flowers.

The boy goes inside. Any conversations between the mother and son are unheard and unknown as the walls of the home hides them.

Jeremiah feels as though he's passing through the part of a dream left unremembered as his imagination explores ideas on what the mother and son may be doing and what may happen next, all depending on what he does and what he chooses. He can imagine the woman and son walking through a house he has no idea about, and he imagines them in the kitchen talking about what they might do for dinner. What shows they'll watch. What they hope for tomorrow. He can also see the many ways in which he might make himself known to them. A ring at the doorbell. A steady knock until they answer. Questions about what they were doing the night Cole went missing. Questions about what they know. No matter what he attempts to assume or play out in preparation, Jeremiah remains unsure of what to do next, as though there were a proper series of steps to take in matters such as this, but he forgot the important parts.

The sun sets lower. Jeremiah sinks down into his driver's seat and waits for darkness to come. That much, at least, seems prudent.

41

The far off countryside of trees and homes has disappeared into a dark void where the moon hangs. A wind rises, and with it, a wall of clouds comes from the west in steady progression, smothering the night in a deeper blackness that consumes heaven until the stars are forgotten one by one. The clouds soon pass before the moon until a ghostlike pallor remains on their edges as lone witness to the moon's existence. Trees rustle with the continued gusts.

Jeremiah shuts his car door, lifting the door handle to avoid the slightest click. With his eyes remaining on the home, he stays hunched as he walks to the curb, his hands in his pockets and chin tucked. He continues at a nonchalant pace along the sidewalk, as though taking an evening stroll, even though his heart pounds inside of him He watches the windows and front door of the home for any movement.

Continuing closer, Jeremiah coaches himself in a whisper that drops into his collar, "If you don't calm down, you'll end up jumping into the bushes." He chuckles at this as he pictures himself diving headlong into the shrubs nearby at the sight of a sauntering cat, making a ruckus of snapping twigs. He laughs again, this time more subdued as he approaches, laughs as his nerves are frayed.

He walks up their driveway, increasing his pace, his shadow beside him on the paneled siding, cast there by the pale streetlamp where the bugs eat at the light in a swarming frenzy. He continues his way to the back of the home, turning at the gutter and entering the backyard. At the end of the rose bushes where the shadows are deepest, Jeremiah sinks down against the house. He stops there. Thoughts assault him. This isn't what he thought it would be. Whoever murdered Cole was supposed to own a dungeon, some dark house of horror isolated and unapproachable along a crackling mountain surrounded by bats and lightning. He can't make wild judgments. He needs more evidence.

Jeremiah shuffles low, passing the roses and nearing the concrete steps and the metal railing that leads up to the back door. He hides, escaping the curious search of the kitchen light that streams out from the open window in an angled rectangle over the lawn. Crouched near the small stairs, he grips the cool metal rail as he listens to what is happening inside.

The television is on with its calls of humor and automated laughter. It sounds deeper within. Possibly coming from a room just off the kitchen. Jeremiah can hear the boy laugh. A moment later there are commercials. Something about a phone.

"Mom, I want one of those." The boy's declaration.

The mother's answer. "Well, I just may have to go ahead and get you one of them for your birthday. It's coming up soon, you know, and I'm not bound to forget about it."

"Mom, can you get me a soda?"

She must have stood.

"Sure thing, baby."

Her frail figure stretches down through the window in a lanky shadow causing Jeremiah to shy further into the night. He draws his arms and legs to his body to keep away, as though the shadow may reveal his intrusion. The woman untwists the soda bottle. It hisses. A glass is poured. Then another. The refrigerator opens and the bottle is placed back inside. Jeremiah begins to creep closer again, but is startled, his heart jumping in his chest, as the woman calls out loudly, "Do you want some ice?"

"Nope!"

The woman's steps are heard leaving the kitchen again. This time, she shuts off the light as the kitchen is put to rest for the night. Jeremiah breathes heavily, again confronted by his lack of planning. He feels as though he's been asking himself, "What now?" with every simple step of progress, often with not much of answer to provide.

He should call the police.

The thought stirs him. Like sitting up from a dream. He tells himself to end this vigilante nonsense. Just call the police. This isn't his place. His role. He should call the police and tell them about the woman and her boy. Tell them to search the house. Tell them.

While searching his back pocket for his phone, Jeremiah stops himself. It would just be more of the same from the police. They'd dismiss his claims. They'd have excuses. Why they can't. Why they won't. Some other failing to offer. If anything, Jeremiah would probably have charges pressed against him for trespassing, along with a litany of other things. Would the police really investigate a puny woman and her teenage son because of the deranged conclusion of a damaged father? No.

Ensuring the phone is on silent, Jeremiah returns it to his back pocket, sorry for the numerous calls he has missed from his wife. Bri. He imagines her with the phone to her ear, pacing back and forth in the kitchen with Abigail in her arms as she tries to remain calm. Bri. He almost leaves, just to go to her and his children.

The boy laughs, waking Jeremiah from his thoughts. Resolved, Jeremiah needs to confront these two. Search the home. Find evidence. Then he can call the police, and whatever ramifications there are for his part, he'll willingly take them. He must find something. It's what Cole deserves.

Jeremiah hunches down until he's a ball of knees and elbows going slowly up the steps. He reaches up for the screen door. It opens with flimsy sounds. Remaining low with the screen door resting at his spine, Jeremiah turns the doorknob slowly. It's unlocked. The door glides open while providing Jeremiah a slim enough entrance to slide through. He closes the door behind him. He hushes himself, now in their kitchen.

Flashes from the television fill the living room, light prancing at the edge of the kitchen and near the dark corners in varied rhythms of illumination. The boy chuckles at something. The woman does too. Jeremiah can't see them. He's thankful for that, knowing they cannot see him.

Jeremiah skims across the linoleum floor, staying small enough to ensure the wall divide keeps him concealed. Inches from the refrigerator, he has to calm himself again after doubts plague his will. Jeremiah tells himself that he's gone too far, that he should turn and leave as silently as he entered, because it's not these poor simple people. It's over. It's time to go back home to his family.

"Mom, that little boy is super-duper handsome," Mike declares as he regards some actor on the screen.

"That he is," Geraldine agrees casually.

"I like him."

"He's quite handsome to be sure."

"Do you think we could bring him to our house?"

Jeremiah stands tall as he rises in his knowing and in his rage. He presents himself in the open doorway before them as shadows darken every crease and hollow of his face. His figure monstrous.

They freeze. Staring like critters.

42

Jeremiah coaxes mother and son into the kitchen with rigid promises that if they simply do what he says, then they won't be hurt. Mother and son offer little resistance, deciding to remain calm as they offer their own promises that everything is okay and it's all a misunderstanding. The two of them sit within their own chairs within their own kitchen. Their wrists and ankles are duct taped firmly as Jeremiah secures them to the chairs. Jeremiah tests the secure nature of their bondage. He pulls up and down and left and right. He's content.

Standing before them, Jeremiah asks, "Did you take my son?"

The boy looks at his mother for leading, but Jeremiah points at him, "Keep your eyes on me."

The woman asks, "What's this all about?"

"Why'd you tie us to our chairs?" the boys asks as he continues to glance back and forth at his wrists.

The woman begins to open her mouth again, but Jeremiah interrupts her. "When I picked you up in the rain, you seemed nice enough. We helped you. And then my son went missing. Did you take him?"

"What is he talking about, Momma?" The boy asks, his simple eyes wide and questioning. Fear in them.

"It's okay, baby, he's upset. The man is just upset is all and trying to find answers. We can't blame him though. He's upset, and we need to try and help him. We should pray for him."

"Don't," Jeremiah says. He repeats again with a shake of his head and a closing of his eyes, "Don't."

"We can help."

"Be quiet," Jeremiah warns.

She gives up such attempts, seeing their futility. Her chest relaxes, her shoulders loosening in their sockets. She looks around the kitchen briefly, planning and thinking with her glances.

Jeremiah is unthreatened by her searching. He leans back against the dirty counter with crumbs sticking to his palms. He brushes them off, scattering them to the floor. He explains, "When the police told me where they found my boy, over by the marsh, I forgot all about you, even though it was right near where I picked you up that day. I should have realized, or at least thought of you. But when I saw your car again this morning at that same gas station where I dropped you, I knew it was you." He accuses again, an answer and a realization far too late, "I knew it was you."

"What's he talking about, Momma?" The boy's voice twangs with panic.

"Shhhhh, baby, shhhhh," she hushes.

"I don't expect you to tell me the truth," Jeremiah affirms. "I already know. It's too perfect. My small son. His missing. His brutalized, raped, beaten, strangled, molested body." His voice constricts. "And I know you did it. You seem innocent enough. But you're not. I can see it. I'm going to look through your house. It's not going to take long. It's not like I'm a detective." Jeremiah laughs out loud at the remembrance of the detective in charge, Detective Jamison, and he pictures her as a Charlie Chaplin of sorts, flopping around in her buffoonery as she shuffles side to side with hands out at her thighs while trying to find clues and stumbling over herself as she does. He says, "I'm going to tear through this house, looking for something, anything. When I'm done, I'm going to call the police, and you're both going to prison. I'll make sure of it."

Jeremiah tests their bound wrists and ankles once more before going into the next room.

The living room is square and tidy, swept and clean. The half-full soda cups sweat onto the coffee table. The television continues to amuse the empty furniture and open room as the news people talk about the local football team which is doing great and really showing promise with a gifted quarterback and solid coaching. Jeremiah turns it off with a click of the old fashioned knob. He moves to the center of the circular throw rug with its alternating blue and white circles growing smaller within. Its edges tattered. Threads unraveling and stains within. Jeremiah looks over the worn away furniture, the coffee table and the tall lamp in the corner turned off and tilted against the wall. He begins walking near the walls, pressing his palm on paneling and poking at soft spots until traveling every inch. He peeks beneath the couch and lifts the cushions. Checks beneath the rug. Touches his feet at each and every floor board. He's not sure what he's expecting to find. A trap door maybe. A latch with a thick metal lock.

There's a door on the wall behind the couch. It looks like a closet. He walks to it. There's the smell of urine, it's source uncertain. His heart rate rises and pumps in his veins with nervous blood. The knob is inches from his outstretched hand before he stops himself, afraid at what horror might be behind, possibly a child gagged and shackled. Maybe a dead boy. He pulls it open slowly. His eyes squint with a wince of expectation. Coats and boots and flannel shirts.

Jeremiah sifts through, searching for some clue or for something out of place – coat sizes that don't belong, or a remnant of his son or some other child. He smells each of the articles. Investigates pockets. Shoves his hands down sleeves. To be sure of no secret door or a hidden away cubby, Jeremiah takes the coats and slings them over his shoulder, scattering them over the floor and furniture until the closet is bare but for a few tarnished coat hangers that swing crookedly.

Jeremiah turns to face the dissected room, looking over it one more time. He can see the mother and son sitting, the mother testing the duct tape at her wrists and ankles cleverly as she seems to coach the boy with words. She's not going anywhere. With the downstairs cleared, Jeremiah hesitates at the bottom of the stairway, left foot on the first step, as he scans around to ensure there's nothing he's missed, some other door, some board or paneling that doesn't match. He's gone through everything he can see.

The stairs creak with Jeremiah's weight as the skin of his palm slides atop the wooden railing in gradual ascent. He tests each step for any irregular sound, something hollow or a creak. At the top, he stares down the hallway of the second floor. Yellow walls. Brown carpet. Four white doors closed shut. He scans the ceiling for an attic door. There is none. He walks to the door nearest him on the left. He pulls it open, still wary. Heart pounding. Stuffed towels, sheets, and other linens litter the shelves of the small closet. He pulls out everything one by one, flattening and inspecting each article before his face. He looks for blood or stains or some other telling, and he tosses each aside when finished, at times taking a moment to scrutinize a stain further until tossing the contents into a disheveled scattering behind him.

He moves further. In the entrance of the bathroom, he pauses in disbelief at the mess of bottles and containers, empty or open, closed or full, and drips of different color and texture and use. The mess is strung out over the sink, covering its surface and dispersed across the floor, some knocked over and some standing. "At least it smells clean," he comments to no one in particular. The oval turquoise rug squishes under his feet as he stands at the sink. He dips his head for a glimpse beneath, pulling out everything and knocking over bottles to search the cool moist corners. He stands again. He kicks some bottles. Checks behind the toilet. The shower curtain is filmed with brown tainted splotches that press up and out in consuming smears that hide the tub behind and anything grotesque that might be there. Jeremiah peels the shower curtain back. Shampoo bottles. A bar of soap. Strands of hair plastered to the blue tiled wall. A pile of soggy hair clumped together at the drain.

He shuts the door as he leaves. Two more doors to go. He's feeling like a failure. He treads over the sheets and towels, the mess of his own creation, as he moves deeper down the hall. The next door swings in against the adjacent wall as he pushes it open. Posters of Pokémon, Spider-Man and Iron-Man decorate the room. A sturdy dresser to the left. A twin size mattress on the opposite wall near a window where blue curtains are drawn shut. The blanket and sheet on the bed are folded down neatly. The tidy room presents itself well, as though the boy has made the choice to be better than the filthy ways of his mother.

At the dresser, Jeremiah opens the top drawer. Underwear and socks are folded and organized. He rummages through, then pulls the drawer out and throws it against the nearby wall, inadvertently gashing a hole into a poster as it hits and falls. The other drawers hold shirts and pants, long sleeved and short, jeans and sweatshirts, all of them age appropriate for the boy, and Jeremiah throws each drawer into the same pile behind him, harder each time with his mounting ire. At the bed, he throws the mattress off its end with a grunt, causing it to lean at a disheveled angle against the wall where another poster rips down. Knees to the ground, Jeremiah ducks his head beneath the bedframe, as a child might do to check for the Boogieman before sleep. Nothing is there, nothing but shoes tucked away in the corner shadows like cowering things hiding from the loud bangs and noises Jeremiah has been making.

Jeremiah stands and kicks the bedframe. It hurts something fierce as the unmoving wood smashes his toes and he curses at the throbbing. He curses himself. Leaving the bedroom, Jeremiah kicks at the clothes along the floor, scattering them as he exits. He kicks some towels in the hallway.

He returns to the top of the stairs, yelling down with a threatening call of, "I'll be back down in a minute!" His words echo back from the empty descending walls, mocking him and his lack of finding, as if the house itself might be defending the innocence of its residents. Walking to the last door, Jeremiah drags his feet over the carpet like a man defeated or condemned.

Jeremiah flicks the light on to the last bedroom. The dim illumination of a dull orange light pours along the walls with a dirty hue that colors Jeremiah the same. The bedroom is the mess he anticipated. Piles of clothes on the unseen floor. Crumpled blankets tossed aside. The sheet on her bed undone so that half the mattress is bare, sweat stains seen in dark filmed splotches. There are half-drunk bottles of soda and Styrofoam food containers on the floor. Some in piles and some scattered. A couple of flies buzz through the air. Jeremiah takes a step further in, and the smell of the room is potent with the woman's period, her blood even visible in the panties nearest him on the floor. He gags. Pinches his nose. Jeremiah scatters and thins out the clothes and things on the floor with the prodding tip of his shoe, but discovers nothing. At the dresser, Jeremiah pulls open drawers constructed in crooked angles – each nearly empty but for parcels of clumped up clothing. When he's done with the bottom drawer, Jeremiah grabs the back edge of the dresser and flips it to the ground, hopping back to avoid the heavy fall as it thuds and shakes the floor. He flips the bed. Nothing.

He sits on the empty bedframe. The havoc of his making before him. The home has been searched. He's found nothing but their innocence. He's not sure what to do next.

He should have just gone home.

Jeremiah feels as though he could sit here for days, pass away in some lonesome death. His forehead drops into his open palms, dark hair over his fingers. He considers himself a fool.

He needs to set the two of them free and apologize. Maybe they'll forgive him after he explains the frailty of his state. Maybe she'll even pray for him as she offered. Or maybe they'll call the police. It's what he deserves.

He hopes Bri isn't too disappointed. He hopes she'll understand. He wonders if he'll ever have to justify himself one day to Gavin and Abigail, and wonders if he'll ever be someone they'd ever look up to.

Jeremiah stands, prepared to receive whatever outcome may be his.

A thought and a whisper visits Jeremiah. It tells him to wait. He's forgotten something. An overlooked hint. Something was missed.

Jeremiah returns to the room of the boy. Walks to the bedframe. This time, he lifts the weighty wood from the floor and tilts it against the wall as best he can, propping it up at an angle. He looks down at the shoes pressed back against the corner. They're small. Jeremiah reaches for a pair of blue ones. He lifts the tongue. There's a "C" written on the size label. Jeremiah presses the shoes to his chest and closes his eyes, embracing the shoes as he whispers out in wounded sadness, "Cole."

43

The boy flies toppling forward after Jeremiah kicks him in the back. Still strapped to his chair, the boy's face smashes against the linoleum. Blood bursts from the boy's lips and teeth as the floor collides with his mouth. With his face turned and pressed against the floor, he cries out with blood in his words "Momma!" as he coughs in pain and starts to cry.

Reaching down over the boy's tumbled shoulders, Jeremiah snags a fistful of thick curly hair, clenching hard as he rips the boy back to the four standing legs of the chair. "Owww owww owww owww!" the boy shrieks while raised to his place. His chair wobbles back and forth with the force as Jeremiah walks back in front of them both.

"Who did this?" Jeremiah demands.

"Did what?" the woman asks.

Jeremiah places Cole's shoes onto the counter behind him before hurling the other shoes at her one by one. Four shoes. Two other lives. Children. She's hit directly in the face by the first, then she shies away as the other shoes bounce off her head and torso.

"I'm going to call the police," Jeremiah announces in conclusion, the matter final. With the shoes as evidence, there's no judge who wouldn't drop the gavel in judgment, no jury who wouldn't convict. He pulls his phone from his pocket. He's missed numerous calls, all from Bri. He can explain later.

He begins dialing 9-1-1 when the old woman cries out, "It's not his fault! It's not Mike's fault! Please, just you wait! Just you listen to what I have to say before you call anyone!"

His fingers hold. "What?" he asks, seething.

"It's not my boy's fault," she says again as she looks over at her son, blood swelling in patches on his lips and cheek, a purple lump forming on his brow. The boy lowers his chin, as if his mother is about to explain an embarrassing symptom to a doctor. "My Mike, he's been abused. He has. It's not his fault what he is. He was abused by my daddy. Please. Just listen! His grandpappy – my daddy. He would abuse him when I sent him over there. I was working three jobs, being single mom and all, and I needed someone to watch Mike. I never would have thought. Mike was only five." She shakes her head at the reality of it. "I didn't know. Please!" She can see that she has Jeremiah's attention, his finger still near the phone, and she continues in a more measured pace, "When I found out what my daddy had been doing, Mike was six years old. Mike had been there one full year having that done to him. One full year if you can believe it! One year of being molested and touched by that monster – my daddy – every night. The only time my boy had a break was when his older cousin would come over, my sister's daughter. She was about twelve or so, bless her soul. That poor girl got the worst of it, being what my daddy preferred, a blond girl and all, but at least my boy got himself a break from it when she was there. I didn't even know. I was so busy working. Didn't see the signs. My daddy never touched me growing up. He touched on a neighbor girl a few times, sure, but not for too long, not long enough to do her any real trouble, not like my Mike. Not like my Mike. Listen. Please. My daddy abused him so bad and it ain't his fault."

Jeremiah asks, not really knowing why, but sad and entangled, "What happened to her?"

She pauses. Questioning. "Which one?"

Her question sickens him. "Your sister's daughter. The girl."

"I'm not sure. I do believe she got hooked on that methamphetamine or something like that when she done turned a little older, selling herself and what not, bless her heart."

"I'm sorry to hear that," Jeremiah says.

She's encouraged by his comment, emboldened even, seeing that the man before her is good enough to sympathize with damaged souls, and she continues, "Mike changed when he was there. Anyone would have with how my daddy touched and hurt him. You know, I drank a lot when I was pregnant with Mike, I admit that, I do, something I'm ashamed of, but it was a hard time, and it's just what I did. Can't change that now. But it made Mike slow, you know. You can see it a little on him, how close his eyes are, that fetal syndrome thing. All of that, combined with what my daddy did, it ain't his fault. None of it. Not a shred of it is his fault."

Mike lifts his face as if for inspection, verifying her words. Jeremiah barely glances.

"When I found out what my daddy had been doing all that time, I quit two of my jobs and brought Mike back home with me. I cursed my daddy out something awful. My daddy never learned though, died of a heart attack two years ago."

"Did he go to prison?" Jeremiah asks.

She states as though it were obvious, "I wasn't going to send my daddy to no prison."

Mike's head drops again, and Geraldine nods her thin chin at him, telling him to be strong. Then she explains, "But when I brought Mike back, my baby boy, he'd changed. He did. Can't help but change with those things done to you every day. Every day. Ain't no one would be the same. But Mike started doing some things. Hurt some kittens and what not. Touched another child in school – just curiosity though – no real harm. So, I took him to some therapists, them learned folk, so they could fix him. They said he had some disorder. I can't recall which one. Seemed like each of them gave Mike something different. They gave him medication, but that stuff did nothing but make him slower. They done talked to him a lot, but my boy's too simple to really understand those things, he's not 'cognitively aware,'" she recites, seeming proud to get the term correct. "But I could see it, what was in him, and I got him as much help as I could find. The men at our church would talk to him some too, but they said they didn't see much wrong, said he was polite and nice enough. But I still saw it. I'm his mother. I know him better than he knows himself. I worked my tail off to find him someone who might listen and understand, not judge him, but see him for the sweet boy that stayed deep inside him, you know, that sweet boy beneath all them bad nights that changed him, and bring that sweet boy back "

"I'm sure," Jeremiah states, his tongue making words. He feels addicted to it all, drawn to the story like some gruesome fancy of the macabre. He prepares to listen further. His heart darkening.

"Yep, yep," she agrees with a nod. She looks closely at Jeremiah and continues, "But I seen it. I seen it. We were at the doctor to get his prescription one day, and Mike done started talking to some little boy, and I seen it right there. Seen it all and what my daddy had done to my boy." She shakes her head sadly. "He was talking so sweetly to that little boy, and I saw what my Mike really wanted." She leaves the details out, the inference potent enough to provide a picture for Jeremiah as he imagines Mike bending low at a doctor's office while talking to a small child, maybe offering to help with a puzzle as the child walks into the claws laid out before him. By force of will, Jeremiah refuses to allow that child to resemble Cole.

"I had to keep him from being locked away, whether in some mental hospital or a detention center, it's all the same, they'd just lock him up which would do him no darn good. How're you going to lock someone up for something they can't help? So, I began to help him. To keep it controlled. And so, I helped him, I did. Did some babysitting for my sister. But not for doing no wrong, just to keep it controlled, you understand, and to help him work through it until he could heal. To help my boy heal. Then one day he saw a neighborhood boy and we didn't want to hurt none of them, we really didn't. It's my daddy's fault. Cross my heart. It's all on my daddy, you can blame him, because my boy didn't want to hurt no one, not once, not ever. At first, Mike just liked laying in bed with them boys, no harm in that. They were just playing."

"When did you know?" Jeremiah asks.

She asks, "Know that your boy would be one?"

"Yes."

"I admit, after you dropped us off, my boy, Mike, well, he took a great liking to your boy."

Jeremiah says and does nothing.

She continues, "Well, Mike just couldn't think of anything else for days. I'd be doing something, anything, making dinner or watching television, and my boy would be like, 'Momma, do you think Cole would like me?' And I couldn't break his simple little heart, so I'd tell him, 'Sure, baby, but you got to stop thinking about that.' I tried to get him to stop thinking about it, I did. Every day I told him, 'Mike, you got to stop.' Well, he wore me out like he can do sometimes, and then we saw your little boy at Wal-Mart, looking over at the toys, and Mike, well, your boy recognized him and asked him if he liked Angry Birds too, and Mike said, 'Yes,' then I picked him up. Cole told me to put him down, told me you were close by, but I walked out real quick with him, even though he kept kicking me and hitting me and telling me you were going to come get him."

Jeremiah goes to open his mouth, to tell her that's enough and to never mention his son again. He vomits violently, bent over as he retches onto the floor.

"Is he okay, Momma?" Mike asks, but his mother shushes him.
Standing, Jeremiah asks with a sleeve to his chin, "Then what?"
Looking at him, she asks, "Are you going to call the police now?"
Jeremiah can hear the crackling of her concern, her want for the
police and the safety they provide. He promises with a finger in the air,
"In a minute. What happened next?" He repeats in unbending command,
"What happened? Tell me. Now."

"Your boy, every day he fought us. He wouldn't eat nothing, and he
never did stay calm. He'd kick and bite every day. He just wouldn't let
Mike near him."

Knowing the answer already, Jeremiah asks anyway, "Did you
touch him, Mike?"

Eyes shamed and low, Mike confesses, "Yes, sir."

She interrupts, "He did, he did! But you got to remember, it ain't his
fault! My daddy did worse things than your boy ever went through! Your
boy got nothing compared to what Mike got! One whole year my boy
had those things done to him. If you're going to be mad at anyone, it
should be my daddy!"

"Don't," Jeremiah offers coldly, a piece of him almost begging for
her to stop. Remembering the marks on his son, Jeremiah begs a sad
question, "Why did you have to hurt him so much?"

She pauses, afraid now as she sees Jeremiah falling apart before her,
sees him rocking the shoes in his arm as if his boy were there, but his
eyes are fierce, burning through her, and she explains, almost as though
the answer was obvious, "That's what Mike did to all them boys. Your
boy got it the worse I guess because he fought back so hard. But it's a
part of my boy's healing, something he's got to do, like there's some
demon in him that wants them other boys to suffer and hurt just like he
did."

Jeremiah wipes away the tears, then pinches the bridge of his nose
with thumb and index finger as though holding back a nosebleed,
pausing as the waves within him begin crashing vehemently, crashing
stronger as they insist upon his action.

"Are you going to call the police?" She probes.

"Soon." Face to the ceiling.

"You call the police, it's okay. It might be the only way to get Mike
to stop. I know that now. I'm sorry for everything. I seen I wasn't able to
do what I was trying. But Mike, I love him. I don't want to see him in
jail, but maybe it's the only thing that will help him. I tried. I did. I'm
sorry for all he done. I thought I was helping. I wasn't though, and I see
that now. I admit that." As Jeremiah raises the phone to call, she assures

in conclusion, "Mike loved them boys though, despite the things he did. He loved your boy, honest to heaven."

"Don't say that." Jeremiah's chin lowers, eyes closed a moment with the grips of deep pain inside of him.

She assures again, trying to ease away the terrible depiction of her son that's been created, trying to provide her son some semblance of virtue as she says, "Mike loved all of them. He really did. That's my promise."

Jeremiah bursts out in great fury, "Don't you dare say that! Don't you dare say he loved *my son*!" Jeremiah slams his breastbone with a fist. "That was *my son*! *I* loved him! *I* loved him! We all did! AND YOU STOLE HIM FROM US!" He shakes his head in desperate disbelief, his words almost incoherent as they scatter out in sobbing rage. "You stole everything! You hurt my son! My baby boy! You raped and killed him!" He thrusts his hands out into the air to mimic strangulation with a forceful shaking of his arms. "You raped and killed my boy." His voice quivers and drops away. He pauses, bent over in spirit and body as he stares at the floor, blinded by tears. "He was my baby boy," he whispers.

The woman remains frozen, careful in the silence. She's said too much, she now knows. In a moment, she'll tell him to call the police again. Not yet though. Not just yet. But Mike attempts to follow the leading words of his mother as he agrees in his simplicity, "I loved Cole. I promise, I did."

"Shut-up," Jeremiah warns.

Mike looks to his mother who shakes her head with caution, but he says, "I did though. I loved him."

"Shut-up," Jeremiah warns. The tilt of his chin causes his eyes to shadow away.

The boy begins to sob, not understanding. "I did though! I loved him! I loved Cole!"

Jeremiah snatches the duct tape from the counter and walks to the boy still held securely in his chair. Tearing a piece off, Jeremiah goes to place the duct tape over the boy's mouth, but Mike shakes his head, causing the tape to stick to itself. He cries again, "I did though! I loved him, but he wouldn't let me!"

Jeremiah flicks the ruined piece to the floor and begins anew with a fresh strip, this time untorn. He starts its edge behind the boy's neck to ensure a grip atop the hairs at the base of his skull. The duct tape unwraps in length beneath the boy's ear and around the curve of his chin, then back around until covering his mouth to silence him. Jeremiah stops. He freezes, the duct tape roll held near the boy's ear as he stands behind him. His mother shushes her son, "Quiet, baby, just be quiet now." The boy shakes his sobbing head as the tears streak down.

Jeremiah falters in confusion. It wasn't supposed to be like this. He should call the police. He eyes the shoes he left behind on the counter, tossed there as he rushed away with the duct tape. He remembers Cole, his son, wincing and choking beneath the strangling grip of this very same boy who sits before him, and can see Cole begging to be released and crying silently in the mud.

The duct tape resumes.

It unwraps in rising circles, layer upon layer, covering the boy's mouth and nose as it continues up and around and over his eyes and to his forehead with tufts of hair just above and then it circles back down until finishing in layers of gray which have consumed every inch of Mike's head and face. Jeremiah steps back. The boy rocks and shakes against the smothering, his wrists stuck tight to the arms of the chair, convulsing in futility and almost tipping over in his panic. Back and forth the boy rocks and shakes, his movements more and more erratic as he fights and begs for air. The boy twists his head in a frenzy, his chest heaving in rapid desperation as the chair legs bang in the kitchen with his effort to be free, but the efforts soon ebb away as his lungs lose their struggle. He kicks and shudders one last time. His duct taped head rolls back and forth as his passive strangulation ends and his curly haired head drops forward, falling to his chest as he dies.

The woman cries out for her son, calling Jeremiah the names of the devil, the names of the condemned. In it all, Jeremiah had barely noticed the woman's shrieks and screams as her shrill cries echo out through the open window, and he's certain someone by now has called the police. He's not sure what that will look like.

"You killed my baby! You killed my angel! You're going to burn in hell for what you did! You're going to burn in hell!"

Jeremiah lays deaf and heartless eyes upon her.

"Burn in hell!" she screams.

Jeremiah grasps her shrieking mouth in his open palm and lunges past her body, taking the momentum and whipping her skull into the hard corner of the counter where the back of her head cracks. She goes limp, thumping to the floor in a bundled heap. Blood expands in a growing pool along her linoleum floor from her broken skull.

Jeremiah holds still. He feels numb. His hands are out from his body, as if unsure of what just happened as he stands between the two dead bodies with the silent pronouncement of deeds done.

Blue and red lights flash as they revolve through the neighborhood, drawing closer to the home. Jeremiah walks to the counter and picks up his son's shoes, carrying them in his curled arm. He sits at the kitchen table in the lone empty chair and scribbles a note on a pad of paper. Finished, he opens the cabinet beneath the sink and finds a trash bag. He drops the shoes and note inside. He ties it shut. The screen door slams behind him with a loud clack as the tight springs swing it closed against the frame. Walking to the front of the house, Jeremiah wonders what he'll say. It's drizzling outside.

44

Red-blue, red-blue, the dense dark of night is wreathed with the alternating colors as they spin in the rain, revolving over the house and trees, the fence and bushes. Standing in the wet grass, Jeremiah winces against the bright contrast as the colored lights pass over his face. A flashlight is pointed at him. Yells are heard. Jeremiah puts a hand up against the flashlight, revealing the blood on his hands and the splattering on his sleeve.

The police officer screams from behind the trunk of the cruiser, calling for Jeremiah to get down. Jeremiah takes a step forward for presentation as the trash bag in his hand crinkles out the sound of the droplets atop it, which are now falling steadily heavier. The officer commands again with growing intensity, but Jeremiah has no interest in listening. He's overwhelmed with what has been done and what it means for him and his family. He cannot return home. He's done something he shouldn't have. His family will suffer because of it.

Jeremiah slings the trash bag towards the car. It ricochets off the trunk and into the officer who shies away as it bounces against him. The officer screams for Jeremiah to get on his face with his hands on his head and to do it now.

Jeremiah steps closer. He's so weary of words. So weary of people. No one ever listened. No one was there when he begged for help. No one cared. He wants to go home. That's all. See his family. Now he can't. He may never go home again. He shakes his head in a fit as tears mix with the rain on his face, and Jeremiah pulls the car keys from his pocket and flings them at the cruiser where they bang metal against metal.

A bullet hits him in the chest. Jeremiah stumbles back and falls to the ground. Looking at the black clouds, the sound of the gunshot continues to echo in his ears. With a trembling finger, Jeremiah tests the truth of the wound as his legs writhe in pain.

The officer is coming in his boots, screaming for Jeremiah to stay down. Jeremiah grins painfully at that. He tilts his face away from the uniform and the flashlight to look at a corner of the sky. His last sight will not be the face of a stranger. Blood seeps down around Jeremiah's torso, drenching the ground with his draining life. He breathes with difficulty.

As the world around Jeremiah disappears, sights and sounds now distant, he thinks of Abigail and her soft kisses. Remembers the feel of her small body upon his chest. He can see Gavin crying when told what has happened, and that hurts far more than anything. He hopes one day his son will understand. He hopes Bri will heal from all he's done. Hopes she finds love again, someone to comfort her as he was never able to. He hopes his family remembers him in good ways. He hopes they know he always loved them. Loved them with all his heart. Tears stream down. He wishes he could at least say, "goodbye."

The last prayer of Jeremiah is silent, held down by the rising blood which fills his mouth, and he prays for his family, prays that God will protect and love them, carry them to heaven when all is over. Beneath the falling rain that caresses his listless body like the pattering fingertips of a child trying to wake him, Jeremiah fades away and is gone.

45

To my beautiful wife, my beloved son, and my sweetest baby girl,
  I love you.
  I never meant to hurt you. I never meant to be how I was for all those months. I'm sorry I was too weak to be there when you needed me. I wanted to be stronger.
  They took Cole, and they hurt him. All I ever wanted was for us to be together, to get old together. They stole that from us.
  I found his shoes in their home. I didn't intend to kill them, I promise. That's all I'll say for now, I can save the rest for when I see you at the jail. Jail. I'm so sorry. Please forgive me.
  Bri, you were always my romance, my love and my pillar, my wife.
  Gavin, my son, when you were born I learned what the word "joy" meant.
  Abigail, no one ever softened my heart like you.
  I have to go. The police are here.
  With deepest love,
  Papa

Bri hugs the letter to her chest as tears of missing drip to the sheets beneath her. Gavin hears the soft cries of his mother and comes into the room.

"What's wrong, Momma?" he asks.

Bri forces a smile, but it quickly falters, and she reaches out for her son and pulls him close, lying in bed as she wraps herself around him.

"Are you crying because of Papa?"

"Yes," she chokes out.

"Is Papa coming home soon?"

"No, baby."

The boy breathes. His chin quivers. "I miss him."

"I miss him, too," she says. Gavin begins to cry in his mother's arms as all his efforts to be a big boy fall apart in the simple love of a missing father. Gavin cries and says, "I want Papa to come home."

"Me too," Bri barely gets out.

The baby monitor flashes from the bedframe as Abigail stirs within her crib, waking up from her nap. Bri delays a moment more as she takes in the warmth and life of her son, the ways he resembles his father, and the ways he's so different. She lifts Gavin as she stands, carrying him with her. Together, they go into Abigail's silver and purple room where the little girl stands in her crib, smiling as they enter.

– The Brothers Series –

Late Autumn Trees
Haunts of Cruelty
The Bear, The Girl, and the Monkey with No Eyes
Coming Soon: *Stain*

– The October Stories –

The Woman in the Window
Coming October 2017: *Nibbles*

www.rscrow.com

https://www.facebook.com/rscrowauthor

Please feel free to leave a review on Amazon.com

Made in the USA
Lexington, KY
11 March 2019